# Love Letters
on Blue Paper

A JOAN KAHN BOOK

# Love Letters on Blue Paper

Arnold Wesker

Harper & Row, Publishers
New York, Evanston, San Francisco, London

For Nanny and Poppy Bicker,
my fond and doting in-laws
and
for Miles, Adam and Jacob

"Six Sundays in January" and "Pools" originally appeared in *Six Sundays in January*, published in England by Jonathan Cape Ltd. in 1971. "A Time of Dying," "The Man Who Became Afraid," and "Love Letters on Blue Paper" originally appeared in *Love Letters on Blue Paper*, published in England by Jonathan Cape Ltd. in 1974.

FIRST U.S. EDITION

**Library of Congress Cataloging in Publication Data**

Wesker, Arnold, date
  Love letters on blue paper.
    CONTENTS: Six Sundays in January.—A time of dying.
  —The man who became afraid.—Pools.—Love letters on blue paper.
I. Title.
PZ4.W5139Lo4 [PR6073.E75] 823'.9'14 74-20422
ISBN 0-06-014561-7

75 76 77 78 79 10 9 8 7 6 5 4 3 2 1

# Contents

# SIX SUNDAYS IN JANUARY
## A long short story

FOR EDNA O'BRIEN

## The First Sunday

On a certain Sunday in January 1966 Marcia Needham laid down the *Observer* newspaper she had been reading and felt an unanswerable mood of desolation and defeat take over from a calm she now knew had deceived her.

The paper's first page had given her information, but gradually moving through political opinions, literary reviews, exhortations to buy this and visit there, summings up of last year's theatrical achievements delivered in the same tones as forecasts for next year's women's fashions, gradually a picture of the world emerged that was beyond her grasp or care and she felt drained of all sweetness or spontaneity. And because of this she craved, like a pregnant woman with sudden desires for tastes long forgotten, to commit an act she had not calculated, to find a face that was not watching or meet eyes which were not on guard, to lose sophistication and discover longings which no sense of guilt could cheat out of recognition.

*I do not feel despair.*

But that was resisting an emotion the times had made fashionable.

*Must stop reacting against fashions; to react against one fashion is to create another; if it's despair I feel then let it be, allow it to exist in all honesty ... But if I acknowledge despair, must I give in to it? We'd change nothing then ...*

3

*Then change nothing, leave time to take care of moods, it always does, moods have their own natural ebb and flow.*

She observed her reasoning wind down and end pinioned and defeated. It was then that she rose quickly and moved away from the chair, the room, that moment, to the garden and her three children who were screaming round a ball.

'Where's Daddy?' she asked.

'He's mending my bike,' said the eldest, who was seven.

'Let's go for a walk,' she said.

'Can I go, can I go, can I go?' The two youngest pounced at her, pulled her, swung on her jumper and implored not to be left out this time. They were sensitive, the tiny ones, to being frequently abandoned in preference for the eldest who could walk in a straight line, not nag, and was good company.

'Of course you can, all of us are going. Coats! Quick! And gloves and a hat, it's cold.'

January days like this in London were her favourite times of the year: blankets of cold and blue mists tucked in the corners of Hampstead Heath; stark trees and the brown of lingering, stubborn leaves; old, expensive Georgian houses painted in black and white and occasionally olive green or pastel blue and tiny bow-fronted shops refitted for selling deep velveted armchairs or the slim-cut dresses of a young and daring fashion.

*Now clothes are for fashion; that's right, that's as it should be; but not thoughts, not attitudes, you mustn't disturb people each year by urging changes of the mind. Only a generation can do that, after they've been allowed to savour them for a while. An attitude must mature. You must face a danger. Tackle it; not stutter around with annually contrived solutions, that's too desperate.*

'Donkey ride, donkey ride,' Jacob and Sara always nagged, while Mark didn't want to ride but he *assumed* it was to be part of the morning. The donkeys puffed and waited and took the three children off. Hampstead Heath was a good place. She knew that now and didn't care to describe it as chi-chi; that was a mean term and had no part in the generous morning mood of that winter's day; the heath was a good place, and the streets that twisted down into the village, scattered with young people in search of breakfast to cook. There was an air of mellow laziness, of satisfaction, filled with the secrets of Saturday night's love-making, it seemed. That was it: Hampstead village on Sunday morning was sweet with the knowing looks of last night's passion.

*And that's how it should be.*

She took the children into a café and sat them down to drink three freezing Coca-Colas on a freezing morning. It didn't worry her that they raged for this drink, so much a symbol of the American lie.

*Leave symbols alone: red herrings to waste your protest on. The evil must be found elsewhere than in a bottle of brown fizz. Fidel Castro almost destroyed his revolution by abandoning the sugar-cane crop. A symbol of Yankee imperialism, he said. Fancy a brilliant man like that succumbing to silly heroics.*

The waitresses who served were hand picked: young, pretty and full-blown. In that moment she almost wished she was a man and felt proud that the girls walked so firmly, swung their hips so lovingly and were arrogant. Her waitress attended the children with care and patience and served her coffee with unobtrusive politeness. One girl wore black net stockings, another white, another wore peach nylons that gave her legs a vibrant sheen, and, noticing the sheen, Marcia looked to her own knees and the large expanse of thigh she revealed. A great sense of her own sexuality came upon her and she squeezed her legs even more tightly crossed, stretched her arms, yawned and enfolded Sara who sat vainly sucking through a bent straw. The waitress brought another straw and, seeing the other children had bent their straws, smiled and brought two more.

'We'll have éclairs, how's that?' said Marcia.

'I want the one with fruit.'

'And I want the one with coffee on top.'

'And I want the *mille feuille*,' said Mark, who could pronounce the words, being the eldest.

They found their way back to the car through alleys and cobbled streets, and outside a church Sara paused by a woman and her stall and said, 'Ooh, look at the lovely flowers.'

'Let's buy Daddy some flowers,' Marcia suggested. 'Wouldn't that be a luxurious thing to do to him this morning? Wouldn't that make him feel he was king of the world.'

'We'll spoil him a lot this morning, shall we?' said Mark.

'We'll spoil him so much he'll think we're madmen, that we don't belong to him,' said Marcia.

'I'm not madmen,' said Jacob.

'I want the purple ones,' said Sara pointing to the violets.

'I want the yellow ones,' said Jacob pointing to the freesias.

'I want those,' said Mark pointing to the anemones.

'And I'll get him tulips and some pussy willow,' said Marcia.

Each bunch was separately wrapped and then Mark said he'd changed his mind and wanted them for his own room, so all of them clamoured to have flowers for their own rooms.

'No, no, no,' said Marcia. 'It's Daddy's morning, prayers are for him today. But be good, be gentle, be artful a little and maybe he'll put them in your rooms without being ordered.'

*Good God, my three young children have a room each, to themselves, for their own young privacy.*

And she felt ashamed to remember the council flats her husband designed for married couples—kitchen, bathroom, dining-room-cum-lounge and two bedrooms, three bedrooms sometimes; but, God forbid, a couple might have three children, or four, and of course they could never have guest rooms for friends to stay with them.

*Careful Marcia, no wasting time on shame. Claim a vision, spend energy there, no point lamenting the past. Don't preach hate or teach shame — too much of that. That's corruption for you, eroding men's sensibilities with jealousies. Don't lead protest up the old confused and vitriolic paths. Gently, Marcia, gently, your children carry flowers for their father this morning; if you should make them give those flowers back, or sleep together in one room, the tragic wars that still went on would still go on. Gently Marcia, that's not the way.*

The last three hundred yards to the car she clowned for the children's delight, staggering backwards on her heels, gasping and screeching, trying not to fall off the mountain.

'What are you laughing for,' she cried at them. 'Stop it at once. Your mother's climbing the Matterhorn and all you can do is giggle, stop it, I say. I'll turn you into pumpkins. I'll get Beelzebub to bubble you in oil.' The children gave themselves up to laughter and staggered backwards, backwards the way their laughing rocked them. 'Come here, come back, help me. Your mother's lost, you laughing hyenas, you shameless baboons, you jackals, beandills, cockroaches, WRETCHES!'

They reached the car and drove home in a sweet contented silence, except for soft breathless sighs and occasional hiccups from Jacob.

'You're drunk, young man,' said Marcia, dragging her youngest backwards from the car.

'It's Daddy's morning, Daddy's morning, Daddy's morning,' and they rang the bell a hundred times.

'You're raging,' their father said. 'The morning's done things to you.' They filled his arms with flowers.

'I've been on a donkey.'

'I've had a Coca-Cola.'

'Mummy's been climbing mountains.'

## The Second Sunday

On the following Sunday Marcia woke earlier than usual, before the children; she had contrived for them to stay up late the night before in the hope they would lie longer. Her husband still slept. Light eased through the curtains and with it the silence of an untouched Sunday morning. She reached down the side of the bed and turned on a record player which lay prepared with Bach toccatas. It had worked as she planned: she had wanted to greet the day with music. How would it be? Would such calculation jar or seem false? She tucked herself back under the blankets, curled on her side, her hands between her legs, and closed her eyes.

Warmth, the knowledge of material security, motherhood and music combined to give her a complete sense of well-being. She curled and hugged herself more tightly. It had worked; the contrivance of it all did not jar, only she felt a little like a naughty child. Soon her husband spoke.

'Is that music?'

'It's music, Buddy, go back to sleep.'

'Where does it come from, for God's sake?'

'I've got the record player on.'

'What, downstairs?' He was obviously slow in focusing the world so early.

'No, here, at my side.'

'At your side?'

'Yes.'

'You mean you just brought it up to the bedroom?'

'I brought it up last night. Now go back to sleep.'

'What time is it then?'

'It's nearly seven.'

Now he sat up. 'Are you mad?'

'Do you want a reply to that question also?'

'Seven o'clock!' He returned into the blankets. But she *would* try to persuade him to share the mood.

'Isn't it good to wake up to the sound of Bach?' she asked. 'Listen, ssh, just listen.' He lay paralysed with incredulity, sleepily obedient to her command, and he listened. The surprise was over, the music gentle and soon he dozed back into sleep trying unsuccessfully to grab at some last strands of the dream he'd just left.

'It's true,' she said. 'And I'm in great need of something that's true.'

'Not philosophy as well, not at seven in the morning, Marcia.' He was right, of course, and she was irritated that he was.

*It's so rarely we make such moments for ourselves, we hardly know any more how to handle them. You're being clumsy, Marcia, you're trying too hard.*

Then she challenged herself, *I dare you to admit all that you're capable of.*

Having confronted herself with the challenge she hesitated to pursue it.

*I'm thirty-five ... Yes, you're thirty-five ... I know I'm attractive ... Yes.*

*I'm a capable housewife, intelligent, sensitive.*

*Yes, yes, attractive, capable, sensitive, all these things; but what can you drag up from yourself that would please, surprise or shock you?*

*Oh hell! Can't you listen to music without lapsing into self-analysis?*

*I could murder* — she thought it simply. *Don't be a fool, of course you couldn't.* She thought again, *I could plunge a knife into a man's stomach* — she felt it as surely as if she had done it.

*No, I couldn't, of course, not unless he was attacking my children, or me, I suppose.*

*What are you looking for, for God's sake, what?*

*I could make love to another man.* She felt no shock at this.

*Though God knows who, they're all so awful, really. Not a poet among them. Handsome, intelligent, gay, wise—the men I know are all that, but not one a poet, not one with a touch of gentle, lovely lunacy. Not one.*

*I could allow two men to make love to me.* That really surprised her. *My God! Could you, Marcia? But wait, do you mean 'could allow' or 'wish you could allow?'* She tried to imagine it. *Yes, I 'could'.*

*I could also die for a cause, making supreme sacrifices.* She thought of Spain, of helping the North Vietnamese.

*How quickly you jumped from thoughts of sexual deviation to noble considerations.*

She smiled mistrustfully at herself and then realized that even to notice the jump was to manifest a deep-rooted puritanism that denied the sexual fantasy. There she was—watching herself, watching herself and watching herself again down these endless rows of intellectual mirrors.

*You'll never penetrate very deeply, young woman. Too self-conscious, slowly picking at your bones. Damn Freud and damn Marx, and yet—unless you can live with them, you'll never climb out, Marcia.*

But at breakfast she was gay and, having made an early start, found that the morning was so soon tidied up she was able to place lunch in a slow oven and make of the morning what she wanted.

'We'll go to Grandma,' she announced; Buddy could be left to his studio. He'd doze, probably.

Her mother lived alone in a self-contained flat re-designed by Buddy and furnished by Marcia with a mixture of modern fittings and bits and pieces from their old rooms in the East End of London. Despite its comfort and the fact that it was still in the area of her friends and comrades, Mrs Newman stubbornly complained.

'This house is old; old houses have bugs.' She was haunted by bugs; bugs on the walls were the horror of their early days in the East End. Most of Marcia's adolescence had been spent in a council flat which, for her mother, was the peak not of respectability — as a Communist Mrs Newman shared little of what was commonly acknowledged 'respectable' — no, it was a peak of just reward. The local council for her was a people's body and flats are built for 'the people'. She wanted a flat as a proof that one could benefit from years of political struggle. But Mrs Newman, with Jewish instincts fortified by political views, naturally despised the petty officials in whose hands lay the sanction to distribute flats; she fought rather than begged the local council and they had not been inclined to help. And so, in her old age, she relented her stubbornness and allowed Marcia to persuade her into a converted dwelling — an unforgivable symbol of the petty bourgeoisie. Even the fact that many of her comrades occupied similar corners of large Victorian houses could not change Mrs Newman's reasoning: council flats were built with the people's money, therefore the people should have the flats.

The children leaped at their grandmother who, tiny and now uncertain on her short legs, was almost bowled over by them.

'All right, all right, so wild, don't be so wild.' She kissed the fast-moving faces that reached up to her. 'Children! You can't hug them these days, no time, off, away, up! Jacob! Leave my clock alone.'

'Hello, Mummy.'

'It's a nice surprise.'

'The children keep asking for their grandmother and since their grandmother won't come to see them, I've brought them to see their grandmother.'

'I've got a home. They can come. This is where *I* live.' Mrs

Newman would not 'go gentle into that good night'. Marcia expected no change, perhaps she even felt sympathy with her mother's views, but the habit of fighting was in them both.

'The centres of family life change, Mummy. It's not easy to schlepp three children halfway across London.'

'Who tells you to live halfway across London?'

'That's my choice.'

'All right, so that's your choice, and my choice is to stay here, there!'

'That's selfish, though.'

'Selfish, selfish! Everything I do is selfish. You want tea?'

'Don't spoil their appetite.' But Marcia wouldn't fight. Secretly she believed that grandmothers had the prerogative to spoil grandchildren. It's the last pleasure of the old and an indulgence for the young — to balance parental control.

'What's happened?' asked Marcia, noticing two half-burned candles in the brass sticks. 'Did you have a power cut?'

'I had no power cut.'

'What are you burning candles for?'

'So I was burning candles.' Mrs Newman hardly wanted to answer. 'It was a Friday night so I burnt candles.'

'But Mummy, you've never been Orthodox, you're a Communist, for God's sake.'

'So, I'm a Communist! And I light candles! Quarrel with me.'

Marcia would have granted even this illogical indulgence, only she knew so well the real reason for her mother's lapse into long abandoned Jewish rituals. It was Mrs Newman's show of disapproval for Marcia marrying a gentile. Fortunately Communism named religion a treacherous opium of the people, and in it she could hide, unknown to herself, her loathing of Christianity as a symbol of Jewish persecution. She would never admit Buddy to be such a symbol, but now with old age her past experiences of anti-Semitism among gentiles in the East End re-emerged and her instincts refused to attribute all insensitivity to capitalism. The religious roots of Mrs Newman's youth fiercely returned and her daughter recognized that in her mother's refusal to eat unkosher meat, in her dabbling with barely remembered prayers before Sabbath candles were revealed racist not political prejudices; and Marcia wondered, would she too grow into a Jewishness she had not been trained to but only knew of and felt?

*I could light candles on Friday night—I'm capable of that.*

North Vietnam, two men in her bed, the comfort of ritual.

*Marx, Freud, Moses—damn them, all three, for the confusion of truths they've brought into the world. But despite their apparent contradiction a reconciliation of those great truths must be possible, must be lived with.*

'Come back with us, Mummy. Spend the rest of the day with the children.'

'And how will I get back?'

'Stay the night.'

'I've got things to do in the morning. Monday morning I've got things to do.'

'What things?'

'What things! What things! You think nothing must be attended to in this house? Who do you think does it? It gets done by itself?' Always the self-defence before the answer. 'I must pay rent and the coalman calls on Mondays. If I'm not here to catch him I'm without coal for a whole week.'

'I'll drive you back.'

'Mind you, it's a long time since I've been.'

'Come on then, coats on.'

'I've prepared my lunch already.'

'Bring it with you.'

'I can't bring soup, look, all this soup I've made for myself. It'll get wasted.'

'Put it in a bottle.'

'Stay and have some. I've got plenty.'

'I can't, I've prepared lunch at home.'

'So? I've prepared mine.' The mixture of sourness and longing was familiar.

'Come,' Marcia embraced her mother, 'come, play with the children, relax. Buddy hasn't seen you for a long time.'

'He misses me, I'm sure.'

'Come.'

They returned by way of Hampstead Heath and had to pause to satisfy cries for 'donkey ride, donkey ride' (again). It was another of those silent, cold, blue-hazed days. Marcia stood with her mother and deliberately turned her face to be battered by the iced wind.

'Are you cold, Mummy?'

'I'm cold, but I love it, you know. Days like this I love them.'

'That's where I get it from—you! Walking in rain, facing winds, kicking my feet in dead leaves. You did it. I remember. You did it and I do it.'

'Of course you get it from me. Who else?'

'I'm not complaining.' She enjoyed the sense of heritage. Despite the rows with her mother Marcia was glad to recognize in herself those traits of passion, madness and humour she most loved her mother for.

'Here, snuggle up,' she clasped Mrs Newman. 'We'll face the new dawn together,' and she raised her head in a mock heroic stance.

'A good place for demonstrations,' her mother observed of the heath. 'I wonder the Party's never held May Day here. Lovely view, bracing, high. Makes you think high. Look, people could gather in that dip over there, not bad, speakers up here. Hyde Park is a dreary place, I've always thought. Always raining on May Day.'

'If it rains there it rains here,' Marcia said pedantically.

'Never,' said her mother. 'Only Hyde Park rains.'

'Mummy, I'm very happy.'

'So you keep telling me. How do you expect me to believe you if you keep telling me.'

'Three lovely grandchildren I've produced for you.'

'Why shouldn't you be happy?'

'A good husband.'

'Only you should have gone to university.'

'A home I enjoy living in.'

'University – and not married so young.'

'I'm disturbed with the world still, it's in me still to be disturbed.'

'You had the brains, you had passions also.'

'But there's a sweetness.'

'And it's all wasted.'

'Wasted? I've made a family. How can you call that waste? Besides, who can know that a university wouldn't have destroyed?'

'What are you saying? University destroy! University gives you books, learning, all that knowledge.'

'Books I've read, you can always read books. No, it's the ideas they'd have shaped.'

'So? Ideas is bad?'

'Bad ideas is bad, you illogical Communist, you. How can you have wanted me to go to a university established by order of what exists to maintain what exists?'

'That's where you're a fool and I'm wise,' said her mother with great pleasure. 'Because in this country we've forced capitalism to be so liberal before it can carry on that it's got to allow the ideas it hates to be preached.'

'And taught?'

'Taught even.'

'But Mummy, that's a massive piece of cynicism.'

'What's cynical about it? Cynical! A word! She throws it around. What does it mean? I said a fact, I made a truth.'

'But doesn't it seem mean to you, to exploit the generosity of a benevolent capitalism in order to bring about its downfall?'

'I don't understand. Mean? Mean to bring down a rotten system? Benevolent capitalism! That's a funny thing, that is. Capitalism – benevolent!' Mrs Newman now began to stamp her feet with the cold. 'Such a long donkey ride they have. They'll be so cold on top of those donkeys.'

The children returned and were all swung down from the donkeys by Marcia, while Mrs Newman pulled and screwed their hats and coats around them.

Suddenly an unexpected gust of wind leapt at them, surprising everyone and lifting Mark's peaked cap off his head and into the air. It rolled down a dip and round a hillock. Marcia ran for it. 'Run Mum, run, run, go on Mum.' But the gods were on holiday and sporting and so another belt of wind tore across the heath, kicked the hat farther away and pounded on Marcia's back.

*It's like that, is it? It's running time, is it? Games then.*

She imagined herself, Walter Mitty-like, to be a runner in the Olympics. By now she was out of sight chasing the stupid cap, but really it was no longer the stupid cap that mattered because, finding herself in motion, she was, as she had not been for a long time, conscious of legs, limbs, movement and a great power she had forgotten could come from her lungs. Suddenly, mad, she screamed, hoisted her skirt, jumped a ditch and ran on past the cap unable to resist the impulse of flight and oblivious of the children and mother she left behind.

*I've not done anything as delicious as this for years.*

She ran and ran, pushing her legs in front of her, forcing them into speed.

*When did you last do the unexpected? When did you last surprise*

*yourself? When did you last do anything demanding the full aggressive*
*power of your body?*

She screamed again, jumped another ditch, stumbled and
finally collapsed in the grass.

*Now that was silly. Just listen to your heart. You can hardly*
*breathe. And your head, it's pounding.*

*It's lovely. Lovely, lovely, lovely.*

*But your body can't take it, fool.*

Now her knees were weak, shock was setting in; she was
embarrassed and looked round to see if anyone had been watching.

*Gently, Marcia, gently. That's the second impulse you've surrend-*
*ered to—Bach at seven in the morning and a race your body can't*
*really take.*

'We saw you,' said Mark, guessing at the indiscretion. 'You
did look funny, Mummy.'

Mrs Newman nodded a knowing head at her daughter and
listened to her heavy breathing.

'There, you satisfied? You had a little run, you satisfied?'
Marcia breathed very deeply three times and composed herself.
'I'm surprised you came back,' her mother added; she buttoned
up her daughter's coat, placed the cap on Mark's head, and the
two women, as though nothing had happened, serenely clasped
the children's hands and strode back to the car as though they
had just conspired to purchase the entire heath.

Buddy also shared Marcia's admiration of Mrs Newman's
qualities, but he was also intimidated by her, as he was so often
by Marcia. A combination of the two women in the house
presented such a powerful atmosphere of maternal passion that
it was no wonder that he crept through it, flickered in it, and
often ran from it, barely concealing his awe. It was that feeling
of gentile inferiority which he and so many gentiles assumed for
themselves as an apologetic mark of respect for a suffering their

race had perpetrated. In certain gentiles this feeling was a humble and disturbing acknowledgment of an historical fact they happened to have lived through; in others it became an obsequious intellectual game, a tragedy reduced to a cult, like articles in Sunday papers written as hymns in praise of a music-hall artiste. Some even learnt Yiddish. Mrs Newman and her daughter sensed these attitudes at once, as children know when they're being talked down to or as adolescents suspect adults twice their age who enjoy the same music they enjoy. Buddy possessed only a little of this attitude. Just enough for Mrs Newman to despise him and sufficiently innocuous for Marcia to forgive him.

It was after lunch on that second Sunday in January, when a finely seasoned three-course meal had been eaten and they all felt over-fed, when dishes for what seemed a hundred guests had been slowly washed and dried and carefully tucked on shelves, when all three adults had driven the children to their rooms and finally they sat in velvet chairs and reached for massive Sunday papers, then, at 3.30 prompt, it seemed to Marcia that the world was dead. Cold, silent, Sunday-dead. Weekends defeated her, brought home to her the feebleness of her laughter and the foolishness of her questions.

*The fault is not my century, it's me.*

And this last recognition made the low grey winter clouds bring Sunday down upon her bleaker than all Sundays of the past. She closed her eyes and dozed, dismissing news, reviews and all the deft opinions which were carefully collected into print by editors and men whose Sundays surely couldn't be less bleak than hers.

*My mother's right. I've told myself I'm happy too many times to be believed: Sunday was made to discover truths like this.*

### The Third Sunday

There was no *slow* suffering about the third Sunday. Marcia was rocketed from sleep with a sharp wordless rage distilled from last Sunday's bleak defeat. Her husband was unnerved throughout the day, despite being accustomed to the moods he called a woman's-own-and-ageing madness!

'What am I supposed to do? I don't know what it is that I'm supposed to do.' He was full of the impotence a man feels when set beside the silent stormings of a woman he's known for a long time. 'All right, go up, go down, have moments of depression, but this! It seeps right through me, it smothers the house, the entire whole and bloody house. That's not fair, is it? Well, is it?'

'Fair?'

'There! I've said the wrong word again. I'm always saying the wrong word. I've never, never, never known anyone could make me feel so inadequate, such a fool. But I'm not a fool. I'm not, you know. Glower all you like, sit silent, move silently, work silently all you want, ignore me; but not your scorn, no, nor your dark derision, will ever make me think I'm a fool. I've got friends also, men of the world, people I can talk with, and women too, women every bit as intelligent as you. I talk with them. They don't make me feel I'm growing senile. That's what you'll do, you'll make me think I'm growing senile, to seed.'

She gave him his tea in bed, she gave him his breakfast, she gave him his lunch, his afternoon cakes and his dinner of hotted-up lunch-overs, and when the evening came and the children had all been individually tucked into bed she sat in the lounge and waited, waited, waited for the day to come to an end.

In bed Buddy was asleep before her. She could not forgive him that he could fall asleep and show not one current of her mood had really touched him. In such moods she would look at his face with a treacherous despising and think how in sleep it was a dull, unbeautiful face that fell into its own flesh, placidly, with no flicker of a contour one could call generous or serene or innocent or dignified. She watched red patches, which were not apparent during the day, spread across his skin; and then she felt ashamed to be witnessing so coldly such defenceless privacy, and turned away, crumbling into herself and the emptiness of a long night's sleep, to dream.

## The Fourth Sunday

But women don't grow old or out of love in neat and recognizable degrees of time; nor are they anxious to confront their heart's mistakes. So, when the fourth Sunday came, Marcia drew the curtains, saw the frost was hard and said, 'Wake up, the frost is thick, we'll take the children skating on the Whitestone pond.' And sure enough the whole of Hampstead had decided to take arms against this winter Sunday and they found skating, screaming, sledging and much bustle on the heath; and all that day the sky was crystal, sharp and blue. Buddy was weak with relief and gratitude that her mood had passed and he blossomed into husband and father though, unfortunately, with too much heartiness. Skating on the pond, beneath blue skies, their loveliest of children at their sides, he knew this, and knew she knew it, and wondered – what now?

They had made an early start. By ten o'clock, only halfway through the morning, they had taken as much of the exhilarating freshness that could reasonably be expected and done all there was to be done.

*You can only treasure fresh experiences in small quantities; like laughter, too much of which turns sour round the lips.*

It is impossible to visit the heath without meeting at least one acquaintance, and suddenly Marcia saw, standing by the pond, watching with a sharp paternal smile, a man they had known for many years. He stood with his hands behind his back, a peaked golfer's cap on his head, a cigarette clinging to his lips and the rest of his dress a mixed assortment of heavy tweeds, suede and wool suggesting an unmodish approach to clothes that was sane and reassuring without being dull.

Crispin Peterson was a very sane and reassuring architect with an intelligence so fierce it seemed to embarrass him. He was known in many countries for he brought together architects, helped projects to fruition and picked the most brilliant students from the architectural schools to place them where they could best develop talents others had not seen. He seemed to Marcia awesome and she remembered thinking him one of the few men of her generation who was unafraid to declare simple beliefs, who suffered no embarrassment nor apologized with false humility for his opinions. Certainly an arrogance accompanied his confidence and earned him the hatred of mean and lesser men whose vagaries of thought he exploded so surely. But though respectful of some he was afraid of no one, not even himself—except at nights, alone, in privacy, where, he once told her, all fears should be kept rather than paraded for men's pity. These qualities attracted to him the inadequate, the uncertain and the lost; though he badly lacked the capacity to succour all whose love and loyalty he excited and had developed a thorniness as defence against those who would suck him dry. He aggressively rebuked and intimidated, and so was left alone, except by an elite of his own choosing. He had only one failing: he was afflicted with shabby irritations and one suffered embarrassment to witness his outbursts upon defenceless barmen for serving stale sandwiches in pubs.

Marcia had met him through Buddy, who had once worked with him on the planning of Hook, which was to be a model town but which was never built by the local authority that had commissioned it. She had been given a set of drawings to deliver to Crispin's office on a day that Buddy had fallen ill with a silly chill that was more an indulgence than an ailment, and, un-characteristically, Crispin was at a loose end. She was terrified of him, intimidated, but when he asked her to lunch she could not refuse. Though he asked about her and lost all trace of his usual aggressiveness, she had behaved that day like a stuttering disciple full of awe and too much admiration, not understanding why she had been singled out to share his time. Certainly there was no question of sexual attraction, there seemed a curiously neutral quality to that part of the man. It was not only lunch they shared, for after the last coffee he seemed to want her company longer, despite that she tried to make it easy for him to dismiss her by saying she must leave. But when it was evening he suggested another meal and, since it was in the days before the first child and she really had no need to return quickly, she agreed and stayed with him, paralysed with doubt that she could be company enough for him.

Marcia never discovered what it was he expected from her. She only knew that in the end she must have disappointed him, for at an odd hour, nine o'clock, he finally agreed that, yes, he should return to do some work, and from that day, though over seven years they'd met sufficiently to call each other friends, she was never again to share so long and personal a time with him. She had been dismissed.

Seeing him now, standing by that pond in Hampstead Heath, it seemed to her that since such an omen of sanity had suddenly, unannounced, come her way she would be mad not to grab it. Crispin slouched like an awkward cuddlesome bear and she knew that his rough kind of purity was what she needed at this moment.

When she called he turned slowly with an amused smile, trying to guess whose voice it was. Then he saw her and strode gallantly up to embrace her and shake Buddy's hand. The first moments of meeting Crispin were like being wanted by the whole world—after that you were on your own.

Marcia was in no mood to pass pleasantries and with an audacity that surprised everyone she said, 'Crispin, what are you doing now?'

'Now?'

'Now, now, at this precise moment?'

'Well, very little, nothing in fact.'

'Then come with me.' Marcia turned to Buddy. 'Darling, please, take the children, lunch will be cooked and there's an apple pie already made. Take them home and let me take Crispin down to the East End.'

'Marcia, what on earth?'

'Crispin Peterson,' she said, 'it's taking a great deal of courage for me to do this so don't argue. I have a sudden urge to show you the place where I was born and grew up, come! Slum with me. No tourist guide, the real thing. I'll show you back streets and hidden playgrounds. I'll give you Jewish food in corner restaurants. Come with me. I'll do the talking. No strain. Come.'

Crispin paused. 'My dear Marcia, what's the matter with you?'

'Go with her, Crispin,' said Buddy. 'For God's sake go with her.'

'Don't make me beg,' Marcia said.

'But of course I'll come. What a splendid idea. You were born there? I never knew.'

*You knew all right, but how well you turn your shock to gentleness. But easy, Marcia, no neurotics. Men are frightened by the sight of women who disintegrate, even men the strength of Crispin.*

She fought off the protestations of her children, reassured them she would see them soon and, clasping Crispin's arm with great affection, she took him to Hampstead tube station where they booked two singles for Aldgate East.

Travelling as she so often did by car made the underground a fresh experience.

'Good God,' she said, 'I'm a victim of such nostalgias.'

'Such as?'

'Undergrounds. I can never travel on one without remembering the war and how we used to sleep down here – the strange smell it has. And I can never forget being with groups of friends on Sundays travelling to and from choir practice. We used to continue rehearsals in the train, full of Jewish arrogance, imagining we were opening the ears of gentile passengers to something new by singing out those great Hebrew chords. Youth *is* a charmed circle, you know. We *were* charmed, and we were charming, too. They were beautiful songs. But we weren't entirely innocent: we used to grin at each other while we sang and glance at the other passengers to make sure they were listening.' She thought about that. 'But that was still innocent, I suppose.'

'You're looking very radiant,' Crispin told her.

'Thank you, Crispin, I feel it. And you're not embarrassed?'

'Of course not. What a strange question.'

'You know, I'm slowly realizing what I've done – bullied you into coming with me. Poor Crispin, you didn't have much option, did you? Now I'm feeling self-conscious and awkward.' She blushed and then laughed. 'No I'm not. I'll resist it. I refuse to be intimidated by you. You don't know you're an intimidating person, do you?'

'Impatient, Marcia. I'm impatient. It's a weakness.'

'You don't really believe that.'

'No, not really,' he grinned like a conspirator. The sight of crowds emerging from the train into the larger crowds at Gardener's Corner gave them both the sensation of an outing.

'This way,' she pulled him immediately down Commercial Street, past Toynbee Hall, towards Wentworth Street.

'Now you're not going to become sentimental, I hope,' he cautioned her.

'Why not?'

'Because that's shallow, that's indulgent and messy, it'll offend my puritanical instincts.'

'You're right. No sentimentality. What then?'

'And don't be coy.'

'Ouch! You *are* making it hard.'

'Nonsense. You're a grown woman. I'm just preventing you from gushing in a way you'll be ashamed of later. Now, where are we?'

'I used to play in these streets, Wentworth Street, Flower and Dean Street, Rothschild Buildings. Here, down here.' She took him down the basement stairs of a 'dwelling for the poor' and through a dim passage which finally led into a large play-ground. The backs of four, gloomy Rothschild tenements surrounded and towered above this playground and kept it hidden from passers-by.

'Isn't it hideous? Like the inside of a prison. But the principle is sound, we all played here, away from the streets. The shape forced intimacy and friendship, and that friendship survived even the bleakness of these dirty walls. Is that being sentimental? I'm not sure; it's just that I'm surprised, constantly surprised that I'm the product of all this. And I'm pleased too. I don't think I'll ever quite get used to the idea that, being what I am, living where I do, I was born here of wide-eyed, green and humble parents. It's not pride. I'm not proud of what I am; after all, what am I? I'm not important, not even a professional lady; but still, I feel something, something satisfies me, what is it, do you think?'

'Change, Marcia. The knowledge of the possibility of change, that's what pleases you.'

'No, change is depressing, sad, surely?'

'You're confusing change with growing older; growing old is sad, it's not the same thing.'

'And this is where I lived.' They had moved round the corner into Fashion Street, narrow, mean, but now choked with cars. 'Here, No. 43. Right at the top. Two rooms and a kitchen on the landing. Do you know, we constantly had those rooms filled with people, and we argued about everything.' She dragged him up the stone stairs to the top which was now vacant and they looked out of the back window.

'Down there are rows of Jewish tailor shops. "Sweatshops" we used to call them. And that's a school you can see, Christ Church—I used to go there. And that church is called Spitalfield Church, and the park by the church is called Itchy Park, and it's all so small now, shrunk. How on earth did we manage?'

'How many were you?'

'Four. I can't tell you what a strange sensation I'm feeling. Four, in these rooms, two rooms, such a strange sensation.' Suddenly she kissed his cheek. 'You know what it is? I've just realized, it's a past. I enjoy having a past, and I enjoy being able to show it to someone, and I'm *not* going to be ashamed of enjoying it. I'm not being sentimental and I know it's not unique, but suddenly I just feel enormously happy to have a past to show someone.'

But once they'd returned to the street and started to make their way towards Petticoat Lane she felt dull and became subdued and silent.

'I'm sorry, Crispin, inflicting my impulses on you like this.'

'You're going through a tough period, aren't you?' Crispin asked.

'Oh my God! How pathetic that makes me feel. I didn't bring you here in order to confide any marital troubles. I can live with my own mistakes, thank you.'

'You're very fortunate then.'

'That was ungracious of me, wasn't it?'

'Look, Marcia, we hardly know each other, but I know how sudden moods can turn mere acquaintances into long-lost friends and that's all right, I don't mind that. And today is Sunday and Sunday is an aimless day and I'm happy to be taken out of it. You may not know me as well as you thought you did, but stop this, stop all *this*: apologizing all the time, pulling dramatic faces and changing from tragic frowns to heroic smiles, it's undignified. Now, pull yourself together and tell me where we are again.'

Marcia led him through Bishopsgate across to Liverpool Street Station. Here they stood at the top of some stairs and leaned on a balcony looking down into the vast Victorian halls filled with passengers running to and emerging from the sub-urban trains.

'We used to spend hours here, looking at the engines, counting the carriages. Do you know,' Marcia began a story, 'the other day I watched a man running to a bus stop in order to meet a bus that was slowly approaching, slowly mind you. There was no one else waiting, I could see. And the driver, seeing that man running, timed his vehicle to reach the post just when the man was ten paces away, and on the pretext that no one was actually there to request him to stop, he revved up and sped on past. Now, what kind of thinking went on in that driver's mind to make him calculate such a miserable act so deliberately? A small thing, isn't it? But it touches me. It touches me so much. It sets off a chain of reactions which remind me of a thousand other spiteful acts and I find it such an oppression, *such* an oppression. I try to remember acts of goodness, I *want* to remember, and I place them alongside acts of spite; but I find I'm more depressed by the mean act than I'm cheered by the good deed. You're silent.'

'If you want me to speak,' he said, 'then that must mean you want to be persuaded you're wrong, and if that's true you can't be feeling as desperate as you sound.'

Marcia sighed. 'Come on, I'll take you to eat hot onion platzels and chopped liver.'

They moved back into the crowds but this time soon broke away across the acres of Spitalfields market, across Commercial Street into Fournier Street and then Brick Lane.

'The Huguenots lived here,' she said. 'Weavers. Weaver Street, Fashion Street, Threadneedle Street, all theirs. Then the Jews came.'

They paused by a small grease-laden shop in which sat a fat old lady who, since Marcia was a child, had sat there making mistakes in the counting and selling of the onion platzels, beygalech and doughnuts baked by her husband and sons at the back of the shop. It seemed impossible that anything could be eaten from such a place, yet everything looked crisp and clean and the smell was rich.

Then Marcia took Crispin to a small Jewish café, sat him down and recommended borsht, chopped egg and onion with chopped liver, and salt beef with latkes.

Just as a fresh wave of relaxation settled on their meal the door of the café was abruptly opened and a slim young woman entered; she seemed to have opened the wrong door, but then resigned herself as though every door she opened would be the wrong one. At first she was uncertain whether to stay, and then appeared sorry to have made the decision to come at all. Her coat was of brown suede, sombre and severely cut, with a high mandarin neckline giving her the appearance of an earnest young commissar. It was only when you looked closely at her that you realized her eyes were mournful and not eager, that her coat was elegant and not harsh. Marcia saw her and called her.

Katerina Levinson came to their table and smiled a slow, apologetic smile.

'How strange, I'd no idea I'd meet anyone I knew.'

'You see?' Marcia turned to Crispin. 'We all keep coming back. Katerina Levinson – Crispin Peterson.'

'Are you the architect behind the Hook project?' Kate asked.

'There were many of us – the town that we never built. Typical.'

'Are you working on anything for us now?' Kate tried to appear interested but failed so obviously that Crispin became irritated.

'I'm going to advise on a new town in Yugoslavia.'

'Giving up England?'

'Resting, rather. It's all so sterile here, or do you approve of the clean, crisp lines of modern architecture?' Crispin dared her to answer.

'I like the Hammersmith flyover, I hate the Shell building; I like the G.P.O. tower, I hate the Roehampton Flats – is that what you want me to say?' Kate battled half-heartedly, knowing she'd irritated Crispin, wanting to apologize but finally not caring.

'Good, that's sound enough.'

'How stern you are, Mr Peterson.'

'I prefer to make no conversation rather than have the tail ends of your attention.' But Crispin softened, realizing something disturbed her. 'Well, look at it, English architecture! Coventry Cathedral! With a canopy like the entrance to an airport, and all those thousands queueing up to see it.' He looked from one to the other of the two women and discovered a similarity in their silence, as though they had arranged to meet in this little café, this street, this area where both had been born.

'You're beginning to make me feel like a foreigner,' he said. 'Look at you, the two of you. Why do Jews suffer as though no one else in the world had ever done so? If returning to the East End on Sunday mornings disturbs you so much then stay away, don't indulge in sentimental journeys you've no stomach for.'

The two women smiled at each other, distant half-smiles recognizing the familiar dilemma over identity.

'You mustn't imagine we're bosom friends,' Marcia told him. 'We only know each other because we live in the same area and our children go to the same school. Isn't that so, Kate?'

'I think I've been in her house half a dozen times in three years,' Kate explained. But they smiled again—they were the Jewish girls born of parents from Russia or Poland, Hungary or was it Lithuania, and they both shared a similar background and a common dilemma.

'Where's your husband?' Marcia asked. 'You see, I don't even remember his name.'

'Abroad. On business. I dumped the children with my mother and fled. God knows why here, though.' She looked around and continued to sit on only half of her chair as though with no intention of staying. 'I don't think I even know this café. Do you?' she asked Marcia.

'Very well. The tailors drank lemon tea here on Sunday mornings. My father brought me, to show me off. And there were other children also, all on parade. But we enjoyed it, being on parade. It's good to have fathers proud of their children.'

'Mr Peterson wouldn't understand that.' Kate suddenly focused a cruel pair of eyes on Crispin.

'Don't be so bloody patronizing, young lady—trying to fit me into your silly myths about Englishmen.'

'I'm sorry.'

'You should be.' Crispin's irritations returned. 'What on earth's the matter with you two?'

'It's Sundays—we hate Sundays, don't we, Kate?'

'The whole bloody family weekend, all of it.'

'Oh?' Crispin could not resist it. 'Is the tale of Jewish family bonds also a myth? What about those proud fathers?'

'Our fathers were not Sunday fathers,' Kate snapped. Then she became ashamed.

'Good God! Do you think those are the signs of racialism?' Marcia asked.

'God knows,' Kate replied, 'God knows about any of the signs.'

'Oh now, come on,' said Crispin. 'Stop all this free-wheeling sentiment, this pausing and sighing and looking for signs. What signs?'

'Now who's patronizing?' Marcia asked.

'You deserve to be patronized, cutting yourself to pieces in public like this. Besides, I'm not being patronizing, I'm just accusing you of dishonesty. Assuming a Jewishness you don't practise and drawing conclusions about humanity because some bored bus driver gives in to an impulse to keep on driving his bus. I should have wanted to drive the bloody thing straight through to Land's End for a bit of sunshine, I'm sure. Tell me, do you cook?'

'Yes.'

'Well?'

'Very well.'

'Do you enjoy it?'

'Yes.'

'And your friends?'

'Most of them cook. Kate does, I know.'

'Well?'

'Most of them well.'

'Of course. And they have children also, don't they?'

'Yes.'

'They're not afraid to have children?'

'Crispin, I can't believe, I just can't believe you're trying to console me by conjuring up images of domestic bliss.'

'Not quite, but don't sneer at domestic bliss. I'm reminding you of a world we're all morbid about and pretend we're frightened of. But are we, in fact? When did you last take a good look at young people, I mean people in their late teens and early twenties? Don't you notice their need for gentleness? Don't you see in them a real kind of generosity and courage—no, don't wince. It's easy to be tricked into being blasé about those virtues but they mean something. Not the acts of kindness to old age pensioners, though even that's real enough, but a kind of openness, an ability not to be afraid of sending flowers to people you like, a willingness to praise and enthuse, to adore your children, a kind of care that's taken. Think about the Christmas cards you received: how many of them weren't bought but were invented, madly contrived? Weren't you surprised how many people actually took time off to devote to them? Haven't you noticed how many friends don't prepare meals for you out of tins but actually plot and concoct dishes to please you? And these aren't just accidental impulses, they're signs, real signs—'

'Of what?'

'Of strength, modesty, faith. You talk of community in the slums and you hanker backwards to a kind of cosy poverty, but you finger your own friends with sneers a mile long.'

Katerina Levinson now entered the conversation: 'I see my friends cheated into engaging their large sensitivities upon the little music of insensitive young men who, when they've sung their pleasant songs, will disappear and leave nothing but a great confusion behind them. I see headlines about wars and famine which witness a relentlessly monumental stupidity from political leaders about which I can do nothing. I see my friends surrender to a facile image of themselves that countless magazines perpetrate—and you expect me to take courage because in the midst of it all they cook complicated meals and invent Christmas cards? You reassure me of nothing, Mr Peterson; you tempt me with the commonplace when I need grandeur, Mr Peterson;

you offer me tiny fragments of normal contentment when it's that very fragmentation makes each part of me stranger to the other.' She paused, and smiled apologetically. 'Let's move, can I rush you, do you mind? I'm beginning to feel claustrophobic.'

They did so, out from the café on to the broad Whitechapel Road, moving slowly past the groups of tailors who seemed strung together by the phrases they spluttered at each other between fits of their chain-smoking coughs. Katerina seemed unable to walk in a straight line but kept glancing at the men, ricocheting from group to group as though terrified she might overhear their conversations. 'I'm sorry,' she said. 'I'm feeling very frail, as though an accident has given me so many bruises I can't bear the risk of more batterings, of any kind. And everything batters me. Harsh words. Foolish, stale, insensitive words. Ugly crockery, unlovely faces, obscene shaped furniture, monstrous buildings. Offensive. So much of it. Fraudulent, synthetic, I can't seem to take them any more, the offences. All of it, offensive. I flinch. I'm sorry, I daren't look at things for long. Don't you ever want to rush away from conversations on buses and trains? Voices hard and bony. Offensive. Ugh! And cruelty. I'm sorry. The knowledge of cruelty. The Auschwitz trials—I can't read them, can you? I'm terrified to open a newspaper in case I discover reports of atrocities or photographs of mutilation. Road accidents, children dying in fires, plane crashes—I can't read them. I don't want any more knowledge of pain, I—I want—I'm sorry.' Again an apologetic smile followed by an outstretched arm from her bent, retreating body.

'What sad girls you are,' Crispin said. 'What sad, sad girls you are.'

Katerina Levinson shook hands with him and fled from them both as she'd fled from her children.

*Crispin Peterson, you disappoint me. You are not as I remember you.*

*Sad girls you called us, yes we're sad. I'm sad. Sad, sad, sad, so much is sad: not tragic, not heavy with catastrophe, just softly lost, delicately gone, a quick mistake.*

She wanted to weep, to hold something in her arms, to comfort and protect some human life. But there was no one to clasp, give love to, only Crispin's arm to which she reached and linked on, suddenly.

The excursion had come to an end and Marcia nearly apologized to Crispin for having used him those few hours.

*But why bother? It will be another six months before you meet again. You've overcome your fear of him, a sign of maturity. Thirty-five you are, Marcia, too old to be intimidated or concerned that all the world should love you.*

That Sunday afternoon the sky turned grey and, as surely, the mood of the household followed. At tea Mark, who took too much relish in his food, grabbed innocently at everything and piled more than he needed on his plate. Marcia, who was obsessional about material excesses, flared into a rage at the thought that such a weakness might take control of her son.

She told Mark to return some of the food and he, having grabbed with more gaiety than greed, refused, throwing his knife and fork petulantly on the table. She slapped his arm and sent him from the kitchen. The miniature man stormed away, hurt at the indignity of chastisement before his younger brother and sister, and ran to the top of the house to his own room.

'I wouldn't speak for a week if I'd been him,' her husband said. 'Must you vent your moods on the children?'

'I vent my love, let them have anger also.' Marcia's eyes widened with anger.

*If we are a weak, indulgent generation, please God let them not be; let them eat peacefully, take only what they want and learn the limitation of their real needs. That way lies freedom, that way lies dignity and self-assurance.*

*But softly, Marcia, watch yourself, Marcia. To rage is an indulgence also. Your quarrel is not really with them, you know it.*

*So what! Must I render myself incapable of any action by constantly questioning my own ability to be right? What can I hand to my children if I doubt and despise myself so much?*

She moved slowly upstairs to make friends with Mark. On the landing, knowing she would come, he had glued to the wall a note printed in pencil. It faced her before she could mount the last flight of stairs, placed in a position he knew she must pass. 'It is too late for you to apologize now,' the note said; she was riveted with great pride and shame to discover her son knew her so well. She found him standing by his table, his features all movement, ready to write another note, ready to continue the battle.

'What are you doing to us?' he asked. 'We all love you.' This final explosion of innocence nearly reduced Marcia to tears. But she hated tears and hated even more to cry and win an easy forgiveness from her children. Instead she reached to clasp him in her arms but he gently pushed her away knowing such a simple reconciliation was not enough.

'Come down and eat then, it's over. We can't continue fighting.'

'I don't want to eat now,' he said, not petulantly this time but with great inevitability. 'I'll eat later,' and he dismissed her.

He stayed in his room for another hour. Marcia cleared away tea-things and then went into the garden to hunt for odd weeds. The garden was healthy, the earth rich and throbbing with layers of mashed leaves from last year's fall, and the young bushes were firm with early shoots and buds promising a buxom spring.

But she did not inspect with great concentration. The incident with Mark had disturbed her, and yet it pleased and satisfied her.

Something was sad and familiar about the way he dealt with her. He was both certain and gentle. What was she recognizing?

As if he felt her preoccupation with him, Mark stood by his window looking down at her working and she, sensing he was there, looked up. They smiled at each other and she waved him down. He needed no urging and soon joined her in the garden.

'Watcha doing, Mum?'

'Messing, really. Pretending I'm working. Getting rid of weeds.'

'Weeds?'

'Well, there aren't many of course, not yet, but they'll come soon enough, and the thing to do is to keep control of them, not let them take over the garden, they strangle the plants.'

'I'll help. Let me help you, shall I?' She pointed out the weeds, warned him not to tear at what he was uncertain of, to ask her first, and they worked together round the brown border, bending up and down, pecking idly at the earth in silence.

When it was too dark to work any longer Marcia took Mark up to his room and asked if he wanted her to read him a story. He nodded and waited till she returned, then they sat on the edge of his bed and Marcia began to read the story of Exodus. She read clumsily, her tongue shyly carving the alien words. She was embarrassed, but she persisted.

*I want him to know, don't ask why, I just want it. I want him to know about the Jews.*

It was this that had disturbed and pleased her – his gentle and sad treatment of her. Now she wanted to deepen those qualities. It seemed to her a tragic paradox that these same qualities and a mellow surprise at their continued survival, which had given the Jew his compassion, had also given him the habit of acquiescence to his own dying. No other race had, with such constant humiliation and agony, accepted the habit of their own slaughter. The knowledge was in her and he too must have it because knowledge of that persecution would temper him. She would not allow suffering to be wasted. The sadness of such dumb and unopposed courage could only be availed in the certain remembering of it, the handing down of it. And when Jacob and Sara grow up they must know too. She would not light candles, nor relearn prayers, but the knowledge of so much dying was their inheritance and must be remembered.

## The Fifth and Sixth Sunday

On the Saturday before the fifth Sunday, on an evening when they had decided not to go out since nothing in the evening columns excited their appetite, the phone rang. It was Harry Levinson.

'Kate's killed herself,' he said. 'She's killed herself here, lying here, dead, for God's sake.' Marcia and Buddy ran to the Levinsons' house. Katerina Levinson was lying on the bed and her husband stood by making gestures in the air, not knowing whether to explain or to ask questions or how to move. One moment he seemed to want to touch her, to move her, the next he seemed about to speak. It was as if he was trying to work out what comes first in such moments. Finally he gave up, sat on the bed and just moaned.

Katerina Levinson had taken her pills and laid herself down waiting to die; and while she waited she had cried, for on her face were stains of dark and dried mascara streams of tears, suggesting that she knew she'd made a mistake but knew as well she'd no more energy to help herself.

The fifth Sunday, then, was the most desperate Sunday in Marcia's life, when she moved dumbly on an edge of sanity. But there was no hysteria and she could not cry. She and Buddy helped Harry Levinson through the details of coroners' calls and funeral arrangements and occasionally that following week sat with him and Katerina's family through the ritual of *shiva*.

The ritual of *shiva* was usually denied the suicide in the Jewish race — God alone could take a man's life, man could only take the life of his neighbour. But Harry Levinson hysterically insisted that he wanted to keep his sad, dead wife company and sat out those six days unshaven, unwashed and uncared for.

All that Sunday Marcia did not eat, neither did she smoke or drink. There developed in her an aversion to have anything touch her. She did not want to feel food in her mouth or have it rest in her stomach. She avoided her children and certainly could not stand to have Buddy breathe a kiss even on her cheeks. Physical contact of any kind choked her and she struggled to purge herself of anything that made her conscious of her body.

Through the bitter winter days of the next week she pushed open windows to let in cold blasts of air which cut through the suffocating closeness of their central heating. She began her mornings by plunging her face in ice-cold water, at first once, then twice, three times a day; holding it there, feeling the blood knocking behind the skin with little pins, pulling itself tight over her high cheek-bones. Sometimes she held her face under to the count of sixty and once to the count of ninety. And each time she would pull her head violently out of the water, gasping for air, wanting to feel every minute tingling stab of the cold on her. She gasped for air and gasped for smells, of leaves and mould and wood, and she took long walks to tire herself out, deliberately punishing her legs and giving her body an ache until she was unable to stand. Then, when her body ached most and she felt she could faint, she found herself a task in the house, whether it needed doing or not: scrubbing wood or polishing furniture or washing heavy carpets on her hands and knees or turning over the wet and heavy earth in the garden.

Halfway through the week she called at the garden shop and in a controlled frenzy ordered shrubs and bulbs and climbing plants to be delivered to the house. All the bare brown spaces she packed with tender shoots. Some she had chosen for their names — liliums, *praecox*, azalea, clematis; others for the colours and patterns the packets promised — innocent honeysuckle, yellow flowered *berberis Julianae*, delicate pink *palonia*. In an afternoon, digging, fertilizing, watering, she planted fifty different types and stood back willing them to grow there and then before her eyes. During those strange days she barely ate, fruit only, or tea matzos. She needed crisp tastes, sharp; she sucked lemons and cubes of ice; and she walked and plunged her face in cold water and gasped, struggling to be free of something, to be fresh, purged; and she spoke to no one.

Buddy watched feebly, as though his wife were sleep-walking, and rushed his attentions between office and children, cheerfully telling them lies to explain their mother's strange silence and behaviour and trying desperately to show sweet patience and understanding. He couldn't know that such a sweetness and docility would one cruel day be chalked against him. How could he, poor soul, for though he'd married the right woman he was the wrong man and nothing that he did now, nor any offering of love or loyalty, would or could be acceptable. No part but the most mechanical of marriage parts could come within the walls of her considerations. But between his lies and the careful smiles she gave the children they seemed pacified, if curious, for she didn't want to frighten them. Neither did she want to frighten herself or descend into madness. She only knew she must follow this need to feel coolness within and about her and rid her senses of a claustrophobic presence which it seemed in thirty years she'd hoarded to herself, as though every pore was cluttered with the dirt of accumulated mistakes.

On the Saturday night before the sixth Sunday, when she could not sleep, she looked out of the window to find it snowing, and without a moment's hesitation moved into the garden and rocked herself back and forth, caressing the bare skin of her long body in the shallow snow. This she did for three minutes till she began to feel numb, then she returned to the house and made a hot lemon tea into which she poured brandy and five spoonfuls of sugar. For the rest of the night Marcia sat in the lounge waiting for warmth to return, suspecting a fit of shivering might come instead; but her skin did not flicker nor her body tremble, at all.

At six in the morning, waking suddenly and finding no one at his side, Buddy came downstairs to the lounge.

'Fine bloody carry on this, isn't it? Eh? Am I an ornament or something? An ornament or a hired jobber? An ornament?'

Now she knew, nor was there the slightest pause in the words she used to tell herself, that she could not bear her husband. Not the sound of his voice nor the shape of his body; not the conversation he made nor the feebleness of his gaiety, not the quality of his dull generosity nor the whine of his slow defeat nor the way he walked or undressed for bed or sat in a chair or ate or held his cigarette. And more than that: she knew that for her children's sake she would not leave him because it was not in her to do so, and this knowledge reduced and rendered her spirit incapable of growing beyond where it now stood. So, she would retreat, retire, she knew this. She would care for nothing, for without love nothing could be cared for.

Marcia returned to her bed. After sleeping for three hours she woke coughing and prickling with irritability. But at once she was alert to the world and the vivid memory of Katerina Levinson's suicide. An appetite for food returned, and with it numbness and oppression. She would eat now.

Gradually she heard movement from the children's rooms, the sound of their feet running on floors as they discovered the toys they'd scattered the night before; she heard the knock of discarded dolls on walls, of toy bricks flung against sideboards, of bed springs jumped on – the whole dawning cacophony of children's noise. Then suddenly she dropped asleep for a last hour.

At ten o'clock she sidled out of bed leaving a rebellious husband who had refused to move, brushed her teeth and forced her face for the last time into iced water. As she came out of the bathroom she noticed the regularly piled mess of broken books, torn comics and crumpled drawing paper which Sara pulled down around her from the bookcase in her room and, in the centre of that mess, Sara herself.

'You terrible child,' Marcia screamed. 'Terrible, terrible child. Don't you ever learn? Look at this mess. How can you do it again and again and again, every morning. Do you want a room of your own? Is this the way you keep it? Never! I won't let you keep a room of your own. I can't bear the way you destroy. Look at this book, I bought it yesterday. Torn, for no reason at all. Don't you know what you're doing? Terrible girl, terrible, terrible, terrible.' She could not rage loudly or eloquently enough and little Sara waited, held by her mother's outbursts, for the slap that always followed such screaming. It didn't come. Marcia simply grabbed the child, began dressing her and the child forgave her.

When all three children were dressed and Marcia had pulled her own clothes on she made them a late breakfast and sat with them, in silence, eating an egg and sipping her tea, staring in front of her, at one spot, at no spot, deaf to the clattering of spoons banged on table, plates and heads. Only Mark sat watching her. She finished her tea, gave a cup to Mark to take to his father, wiped the draining board — which was unnecessary since she had not even started, let alone finished, the washing up — put on an apron, opened the newspaper, saw nothing, took off her apron and went into the lavatory.

But in the lavatory there was nothing she wanted to do. Instead she looked at herself in the mirror and there, cried. Oh, the terrible pity of that girl's death. That sad face, those flinching eyes and her pathetic complaining, vulnerability. She had killed herself. She had killed herself and had known even that was a mistake. Marcia wept, she tried not to because she felt her friendship with Katerina had been so slight. Why should she cry, what could have hurt her so much? And yet so much was hurting her. Now she ached also; she ached for her own unhappiness; for the waste and the helplessness felt for inadequacies; for the sure knowledge that time passes and desires change and though that's as it should be she ached none the less for the sadness of it and the rightness, and for the certain knowledge of the beauty in the world and that some men never know it but come and go and touch nothing; and for Katerina Levinson's beauty, she ached for that also, and the pity of it and the sadness and the waste and the unimaginable pity of it.

When she came back to the kitchen she drank more tea and sat hugging Jacob and then Sara and then Mark. And all that Sunday she couldn't bear to leave them alone but played with them and sang to them and touched, held and watched them, continuously. Once, in the afternoon, for a moment, she slipped away into her own thoughts until she caught Mark looking at her and he said, 'Come on now, Mummy, *you* lie in *my* arms,' so she crept into him, like a man, and they lay on the long carpeted floor while Buddy saw nothing, and Marcia thanked God her son was born with sadness in him.

*1966*

# A TIME OF DYING

A sort of story

It became a time of dying.

I was in the offices of the *Sunday Times* researching for a play when, returning from lunch one day, I found an urgent message to ring my wife, Dusty. 'Aunty Sarah's in her last hours', she said, 'Della's just phoned.' Della is my sister. I rang her at once to ask if she could pick me up so that we could go together to the hospital. She gently pointed out it would make more sense for me to take a cab north to the workshop in Hampstead (she and my brother-in-law run a firm of shopfitters) and we'd go from there since the hospital was out at Whips Cross via the North Circular Road. From the workshop I rang our mother, Aunt Sarah's sister-in-law, who, though I was reluctant to distress her, would have been angry not to have been told.

The relationships will become even more involved as we continue.

Aunt Sarah's decline began during a holiday in Italy. The first holiday she and Aunt Anne had had since Sarah's retirement from the Union. Theirs was the old story of two daughters who'd never married because of the need to care for an invalid mother. In the heat of that unfamiliar Mediterranean sun she'd had a stroke – mild, but an awfully final and ungrateful reminder that years of active political life were now really over. Retirement was bad enough – who wanted the cosy flat anyway, with its shelves of classics and pink Left Book Club editions, its photographs in frames of all the beloved nieces and nephews and their even more

45

fussed-over offspring, its warm hissing gasfire? But to be struck down as well, that was so unnecessary, so unkind.

Then, two weeks ago Sarah, accompanied by Anne, stirred herself and agreed as an old and respected ex-organizer to attend the Annual Conference of the Garment Workers' Union in Llandudno. The journey and excitement were too much. She had a heart attack. Aunty Billie, the third of four sisters to whom my father had been an only brother, joined Anne in North Wales where together they stayed a week looking after their tiny framed 'Ketzel' until she was recovered sufficiently to be brought back to the Whipps Cross Hospital in Epping Forest.

We'd visited her there on two occasions, taking her caraway-seed bread sandwiches of smoked salmon and recent photographs of the children – though God knows why we imagined such reminders of the good life and of the living would give pleasure to a fading old woman. Two days before the phone call we'd brought Aunt Anne to our house for the night, imagining to give her a break, but the pain and worry in her face told us she would need much more than a night with us to relax the tensions built in her through years of tending the invalided 'boba' and the spent, morose and broken sister. Della had taken her to the hospital the next evening and heard the doctor talk about Sarah returning home in a week. That night came the severe heart attack. The hospital phoned Anne at 2 a.m. but she'd had such a restless night in our place that she was deep asleep from a pill and heard nothing, not even the police who came at 6 in the morning. At 8 a.m. they succeeded in waking her and she was at her sister's side by 9. By 10 a.m. Aunts Billie and Rae together with their husbands Sammy and Solly (who were brothers and also their cousins) had joined her.

At the hospital we found them all sitting on a bench in the hot sun across from June Ward. I reached to kiss Aunt Anne first and she folded crying into my shoulders so that I had to delay kissing

the other aunts. I wondered absurdly would they understand?
Della wept. We thought it must be over for the little Bolshevik
but apparently the family had simply been asked to leave while
the doctors were attending her. It was 3.30.They'd all been there
some five hours or more. There was fatigue and a helpless unhappiness among them.

I was particularly concerned about Uncle Solly, who'd not
long ago had a plastic valve attached to his heart after years and
years of sudden and fearful rushes in and out of hospitals. 'You
know', he once confided to me when I was visiting him in one of
them, 'you agitate for "that" here and you fight for "this" there but
I'll tell you,' his Welsh accent fitted his wise whispering (my
grandparents had landed in Swansea from Russia), 'I'll tell you,
there are only two classes really, only two classes in this world of
ours that really matter, and when you're in here you know them
– the sick and the healthy. No other division among men really
matters, believe me.'

We asked had they eaten. Aunty Anne hadn't but the others
had managed to break away for a bite. There were awkward
shuffles and silences and I resented that dying could make, albeit
briefly, strangers of such a close family. Finally we went in to see
Aunty Sarah. She was propped against stained pillows, a plastic
oxygen mask held to her face by a thin white elastic cord. There
were holes at the side of the mask to enable her to receive a mixture
of air with the oxygen. Her face lolled to her right side. Her mouth
drooped open, her right eye – under pressure from the tilt of her
face – was completely closed, the left one half open. She breathed
in gasps. Such withering. Della cried. Aunty Rae joined us.

I suggested to Della that she try to persuade Anne to let Solly
drive her to a café. She went out and some minutes later returned,
announcing the little miracle that there was tea and biscuits for
everyone; she'd persuaded the nurse to let her make some. Only
my sister could achieve that. We all went into the sun to drink the

tea and then I again suggested they take a break; Della and I would stay. Uncle Solly had done too much rushing, more than his plastic-valved heart should have to bear. I pointed out that Aunt Sarah's state could go on for ages, and the sister confirmed this. They agreed and left, saying they'd return about 8 if we hadn't phoned before.

My sister and I sat by the bedside. Looking at this dying woman I couldn't cry; not until I began to remember her as she sometimes was in their East End flat. Block F, 134 Rothschild Buildings, Flower and Dean Street, topped up by the excitement of having read a new novel or biography, full of stories about union battles. Which led me to other memories and of course to my father, Joe. How like him his sister Sarah was. Aunt Rae had said: 'She gave up as soon as she retired. Sat in an armchair and never moved again. You know they offered her a job, a small job, at party headquarters? She said no. At the time your Uncle Sammy said, and I didn't believe him then but I'm beginning to think he's right now, he said it was Russia that finished her off. She never recovered from the Khruschev revelations. And then she became just like Joe, just like your father. You used to say something to him and he'd say, "Uch! leave me alone." I used to tell Sarah to get up, move about, do things, she'd say, "Uch! I can't be bothered." Exactly the same.'

Aunty Rae and my father were the eldest and twins. 'But if you're interested I came first,' she told me. She can still speak, read and write a little Russian: 'It's over sixty years you know.' So could my father. Then came Sarah, Billie and Anne. There was an Esther and a Zalman but they died as children. I loved to hear the aunts talk about the past and especially I took great pleasure in the names of my never-known family in the Ukraine: Pesha Chaia, Rocha (my grandmother), Bathsheba, Freyda, Modcha, Mendel (my grandfather), Basha. 'When we first arrived,' Aunty Anne used to tell us, 'we had to wait till we could come off the boat, regulations or something. And Aunty Freyda came on board with a bunch of bananas and other things for the night. And of course we kids, we'd never seen bananas before and we didn't know what to do with them, so you know what we did? Slept on them! That's right, slept on them and squashed them and then threw them down the lavatory.' And she giggled. Anne was the chuckler, I've never met anyone who could laugh so much at her own memories (though not these days of course). Billie was the one with the advanced ideas about sex and social relationships, Sarah was the political agitator, Rae the sensible eldest and my father the spoilt, intelligent, lovable weakling. And they all read, avidly, and heaped adoration on the five offspring, Della, myself and our cousins Bryan and Rachel, who belonged to Billie, and Freyda, who was adopted by Rae. Dark-skinned aunts, with black passionate rings around their eyes as though one of the Mongol hordes had once splashed around in our blood a bit.

After some time of just sitting by the bedside Della and I tried to read newspapers. 'Do you think', I asked her, 'that it's possible she can hear us and register what we are saying and can't do anything about it?' She assured me our aunt was unconscious. Eight years my senior and blessed with an almost unnaturally young look of clear-skinned beauty, she makes me feel, in such situations, very much the young brother, though nothing is really young about forty, not even brotherhood.

I watched the line of Sarah's jaw rise and fall as her flawed heart clutched for air. And as I watched it seemed that the gaps between some of her breathing were longer. I asked Della to see if she could also notice it. She couldn't. It was very hot and her period was on. She asked me to go to the car to get her some sanitary towels. When I returned she said Sarah's breathing seemed more feeble. It was. I'd been right. We called in the sister, who felt pulses and confirmed that the breathing was fading. I phoned to Aunt Billie's flat. Solly answered and I told him what was happening. He said they'd come despite them having just, ten minutes ago, sat down.

We sat watching and both now feared it would all be over before the others returned. I stared and stared at the face, this dying, and inevitably conjured up scenes of my own deathbed. There'll be no gentle going in peace from me. I shall resent the living and my end among them that's for sure. And then I had a need to take hold of my aunt's hand, or I wanted someone to hold it. It seemed wrong to leave her so unattached. I was embarrassed and self-conscious to make what I feared might seem a dramatic gesture in front of Della, but I couldn't bear to see her lying there alone and finally took her hand in mine. It was cold. I felt her face and neck. They were warm. It confused me. The nurse asked us if we'd like supper and brought us a tray of veal and ham pie with salad and potatoes and tea.

While we were eating the others returned and we felt suddenly the incongruity of sitting there eating while watching our aunt die. They arrived for what were virtually the last gasps. Billie and Anne wept, Della also. I held Aunt Anne's shoulders and pushed back my own tears. Everything suddenly seemed to be happening in slow motion. There was barely a movement from the lying figure, just a flickering of the tongue. We seemed, all of us, uncertain what to do. Solly called the sister who asked us to leave. We waited outside. After some seconds Rae, Billie and Della went back in. Sarah had died. 'It's over,' I said to Aunty Anne who clung to me and now cried uncontrollably. I could barely find or speak words to console her. 'You'll both have peace now,' I said. 'You've done everything.' I took her to Solly's car and then joined the others in the sister's office.

One never knows what to do. How do you bury the dead? To whom do you go first? The undertaker? The burial ground? The town hall? When my father had died I didn't even want the bother of finding out. My cousin Bryan, who is a solicitor, had made the arrangements. It's strange how, though surrounded by so much dying, death is a surprise. You want to stand still and face the shock, make sure it's true and not be caught up with the details of second to second living. Everything you do seems wrong or sacrilegious: to drink a cup of tea, talk, smoke a cigarette, even the act of walking away from the body. Each movement appears to be a betrayal, a sign of not having cared.

There is in the Jewish religion what had seemed to me the feeble and mechanical custom of sitting 'shiva' – a ritual where the nearest sit on low stools for seven days and do not shave, cook or work. Daughters-in-law, sisters-in-law, and neighbours provide endless cups of tea and food for visitors who come to share the mourning, and they, the visitors, knowing its purpose, bring food with them so that little need be cooked. When my father died I understood the reasons for the 'shiva' I'd scorned: I wanted to be allowed to do nothing, to reach out for an action which showed I cared for him at a time when, paradoxically, all action seemed treacherous. 'Shiva', a time of inaction, doing nothing, then seemed to me well and wisely conceived. But what did Aunt Sarah want? That tiny aetheistic campaigner whose belief in reason was absolute?

I said we should all return to Aunt Billie's, which we did, where arrangements were made. Sarah had said she wanted to be cremated and we discussed plans for this. While we were discussing them my mother had taken a taxi to the hospital but it had been too late. 'I found her lying very peacefully,' she said on the phone, and though they had not been the best of friends in life, despite the fact that both were communists, her grief was deep and I could hear her crying. It didn't surprise me for it had always seemed to me that their hearts had not been in their differences. Neither was capable of the real hatred a bitter quarrel demanded. And now, with the inevitability we always seem to forget, dying made their enmities irrelevant.

Five days later she was cremated in Golders Green Cemetery, in the same chapel where, six years ago, George Devine, founder of the English Stage Company to which I owe much, had also been cremated. It was a simple ceremony, but one which I insisted on stage-managing, for fear that if left to the professional dignifiers of death, her going would be officiated with offensive and perfunctory banality. These moments could be so awkward and pointless, degenerating pain into embarrassment. So, the slow movement from Mahler's 8th symphony carried us into the sombre setting. It had to be a sad entry, we *were* sad, but I was determined we should leave in defiance, as she'd want. Someone from the Party's executive gave her a seven-minute oration followed by one on behalf of her Union. I read Christopher Logue's poem *A Singing Prayer.* Then came the incredibly cruel and long-drawn-out moment when the heavy doors opened and the coffin slid inexorably into what one imagines must be a furnace. It is not, merely a symbol for one. And then Beethoven's *Missa Solemnis* thrust us out into daylight.

After Aunt Sarah's death, Uncle Sammy began to talk endlessly about dying. One day about two years later when I went to visit him and Aunt Billie, whom he adored, he told me: 'Each night when I go to bed I say to the old cow, "See you in the morning, if I make it." And so far I've made it. But not for much longer. Are you happy?'

'I'm happy,' I told him, 'and not happy. And you?'

'How can I be happy? I've worked all my life at a job I've always hated.' He had been a taxi driver. 'I've got nothing to show for it, no money. I'm married to an old crow and I'm seventy-two years old. What have I got to be happy about?'

When my brother-in-law, Ralph, had heard from Della of Sarah's death he said: 'We're going to have a lot of this from now on.' He and my sister took her ashes to their cottage in Norfolk, where they'd once lived the good and basic life and where the aunts had come on holiday, and they planted a tree over it – a flower shrub actually.

Five days after the cremation, at 6.30 one morning, another aunt died, of cancer – the wife of my mother's brother, another sister-in-law to her and another Aunty Ray to me, but spelt differently. She had had a breast removed some months previously but her son, my cousin Maurice, had told me it was more than cancer of the breast – it was cancer, no two ways, and advanced.

When we visited her she'd looked perky and healthy, and as though she was enjoying the friendly fuss made over her by the nurses of St Bartholomew's, which made a change from the fussing she did over others, yet she was eager to get out and home. They released her from hospital and while at home she fell off a chair. She was taken back in, again recovered, and some weeks later they again sent her home. She didn't know what was happening; though once, because of some unconscious insight, she told my mother: 'You know, Leah, I don't want to die,' in that tone of voice which recognizes how rough it's all been but still, she was beginning to get pleasure now.

Tall, energetic Aunty Ray. Proud of every poor possession she'd kept shining and polished for so long against all odds: her scrubbed, good-natured children, the heavy, Mansion-polished, three-piece leather suite, her ability to earn a small income playing the piano for the keep-fit classes in evening institutes. 'And you know what? They say they wouldn't know what they'd do without me.' A woman of innocence and honesty marred by only one dubious act that I can remember: an irresistible need for the special comfort a taste of butter can bring made her sink all scruples during the War in order to buy a little above the ration on the black market.

She was also not a very good solo player. I don't suppose any of us were really but we all played. Halfpenny prop-and-cop, penny a solo, three-halfpence a misere, twopence an abundance, twopence halfpenny a misere ouvert and threepence an abundance declare. And we played pontoon also and chasing the ace, sevens, clubiyash and Lucy. In later years it was poker and canasta. But never bridge.

I saw her twice in hospital. They'd been giving her hormone injections which made her thin and held-high face swell and hairs grow from her chin. Her daughters had had to shave her. But plans, plans! She was full of plans for her return, and about the time of Aunt Sarah's funeral she came out, grateful and eager. Two days later Dusty phoned Uncle Harry to find out how his wife was and to offer help in shopping. He said she was having difficulty in breathing. The next evening, as a matter of routine, expecting nothing serious, I phoned again. My mother answered. She whispered to me through the phone, and so I knew she was speaking from a room full of people, that Aunty Ray was very ill. I spoke to my cousin, Norma, who told me how she'd taken a sudden turn and could hardly breathe. I said I wanted to come round. She asked when. I said I'd phoned to see if I could come in a few days but could I come now. She said: 'Yes, come now, it may be your last opportunity.'

Dusty was shocked to hear that Aunty Ray was in so bad a condition. They had for one another a special soft spot these two – the old, hardworking, upright Jewish mother for the young, hardworking, upright Christian one. Tough stock, both, admiring each other from alien backgrounds. Aunty Ray would click her tongue and, speaking in that special Jewish low and confidential tone – as though everything said should be kept from the hostile 'goy' – she'd nudge me and say with wonderment: 'She never stops does she?' Dusty laughed when I told her, her blonde energy blossoming in this strange, adopted environment she'd fought hard to be part of, and said: 'Good ole stick she is, ole Aunty Ray. I really like *her*,' as though there could be doubts about the rest of my demanding and overwhelming family.

We had to invent a story about us passing by on the way to a dinner date in case the all too-shrewd aunt guessed at the reason for our presence. We left at once and bought a box of chocolates holding firmly to the warm habits of the living.

In their flat was my sister with Aunty Anne. Della had collected Anne to stay with her for the weekend and on the way back had called in to pick up my mother and they had stumbled upon the scene. Anne's sepulchral face fitted the setting of slow-motion bewilderment – except that she was surprised the others could be so surprised about the act of dying, with which she was still freshly familiar. But it was not a normal death scene: we entered in upon a fractured, off-key setting, bizarre.

Aunty Ray was not prostrate in a bed as the dying usually are; instead she was sitting in a chair in the kitchen gasping for breath. Uncle Harry and his daughters, Norma and Thelma, were trying to persuade her to move into bed. She was refusing and there was a curious amusement in the air as though one were dealing with a comically stubborn child rather than a dying woman. Everyone in the front room was trying to behave as though they'd just gathered for a cup of tea, while Dusty and I were ushered through the front room, past the kitchen, into another smaller room, for fear that if Aunty Ray managed to get up and walk to the bed-room then she'd see us, who'd not been there before, and guess at what was wrong. But she didn't have the energy to move and continued refusing to be carried. She was half dopy with drugs. There was an impasse. It *was* funny. The girls smiled in confusion. My uncle just looked confused.

Poor Uncle Harry, my mother's brother; the family came from Transylvania and she'd once saved him from drowning in the river which ran through the village of Harumcurt (Three Wells), though in fact they were all born in Gyergószentmiklos (George St Michael). He was seven, she was eleven, I think. He regretted the political fights with his wife now: 'I blame myself for every-thing,' he said. We always do when they die. But his quarrels were never really with Aunty Ray. I remembered once when we'd had them with us for a holiday in our house in Wales he'd shocked me by screaming at me: 'Don't think I can't use big words, you're not the only one who knows big words.' He'd bitterly resented having had no education and I'd not realized how deeply he felt it until – I think it was while I was trying to defend something Aunty Ray had said – he broke through his normal kindness to rage at me.

There had been fourteen children. Names again. Lovely ones. They were born of Jacob Perlmutter and Bella Toba Cornweildt – my grandparents. Jacob had a brother they called Fatah Henchel who married someone they called Mimah Blimah. The first three died at birth. The remaining eleven were: Sarah the eldest, dead. Ida, dead. Bernard, growing old with his children in Plymouth – the most distant part of the family. Isadore, very old, religious and sweet, living in Beersheva. Minko, dead. Oscar, in Tel Aviv. Layosh, in Bucharest. Cecile (Leah my mother). Then Osha, died at eighteen months. Then Herman (Harry). And then the youngest, Ignatz, known as Uncle Perly, the generous, and only, successful businessman in the family.

Harry, to his credit, had failed again and again trying to launch little businesses in which Perly patiently tried to prop him up – to his credit, but, it must be confessed, inevitably. After all he was a communist. Mind you, not that many communists from that East End era of anti-Mosely demonstrations didn't become high financiers, many did. They'd learned the workings of the evil capitalist system too well. Not Uncle Harry though, he never really understood how it worked, only that it was evil. Ah! Those little businesses of his in wholesale stationery and printing. I loved them. Offices full of staplers, date-stamps, name-stamps, paper-clips, carbon papers, pink rubber finger-grips, white pads.

Who knows but that my first excitement for ink on paper were not stirred by his storerooms of office equipment? A kind man upon whom I could always rely for pocket money.

'That's the trouble with our family', I said to Norma, with whom we were chatting in the small room while efforts were still being made to move Aunty Ray from the kitchen, 'they're all kind. Good natured and kind. We grew up without any experience or understanding of the nature of evil. It's a serious defect, like being colour blind or tone deaf. I bet everyone in our family has made huge mistakes because of it.' Norma countered her grief as most of us do by relating the events of the past hours as though describing an odd thing that happened to her on the way to ...

But it seemed ridiculous, Aunty Ray on the chair in the kitchen, her husband hovering helplessly and on the verge of tears, us chatting in low tones, pretending we weren't there, and the rest sitting anxiously and unhappily in the front room. Dusty in particular, for whom dying was the livelong, recurrent source of terrorizing incomprehensibility, sat absorbed by her own unique and nervously comforting twitch: legs crossed with the top one, from knee-cap to foot, bouncing up and down as though in perpetual rhythm to silently sung melodies.

So I suggested that Mike, Norma's husband, and I lift the chair with Aunty Ray in it and carry her to her bed that way. She protested that she was too heavy and we might strain ourselves. But we were firm and slowly moved the long haul round the corner, stopping every few feet for her breath, not ours, until we reached her bedside which she insisted she mount alone.

Her daughters took off some of her clothes, and all she could do in her breathless state was puff out concerned questions about her family and urge everyone to eat and attend to themselves. I said: 'We've brought you a box of chocolates, Aunty Ray.'

'A box of chocolates? Mmm! Show me them', she said.

I went to bring the impressive looking sweets, which she admired, gratefully accompanied by, as always when confronted with gifts, an incredulous disbelief that anything could be given her.

'You want one?' I offered.

'Yeach!' she replied. Which made us laugh.

She was not expected to last for more than forty-eight hours.

The next morning, at about 7.30, the telephone rang. As it was Saturday, and thinking it was for the children, one of their friends, I didn't move to answer it but tried to sleep on. I couldn't. At 8.30 I went down to make a cup of tea and it rang again. It was Dusty's nephew, Keith, from Norfolk. 'I've got some bad news,' he said, 'Poppy Bicker's had a stroke and it's touch and go for the next couple of hours.'

I couldn't believe it could all be happening. I woke Dusty to tell her about her father. Poppy Bicker had waited years to have an operation on his hip and we all thought it had been successful. The stroke turned out to be the unexpected price. 'Poor ole man,' Dusty wept, 'all these years he've waited to have his operation and now he've got this luck. He thought this'd be his making and it's his unmaking. Poor ole Poppy.' Distress pressured her into dialect.

We decided to go at once to Norwich. I phoned Norma's house where I thought my mother would be sleeping for the night. Deana, Thelma's daughter, answered. But shouldn't she have been sleeping in my sister's house? I asked how Aunty Ray was. 'She's dead,' her grand-daughter replied. I told Dusty. 'Oh my God, no! What's happening?' She sat on the top of the stairs, still in night-dress, defenceless as one is on first waking and she cried. I phoned my sister. Ralph answered. It was my mother not Deana who had stayed with Della. Deana had in fact stayed with Norma. The family had permutated its members, placing together who needed who in crisis. Both Della and mother were on their way to Uncle Harry's flat.

When I put the phone down the accumulation of events hit me – Aunt Sarah, Aunt Ray, Poppy Bicker – and I could no longer hold back tears. My young and very surprised daughter, Tanya, who was near me by the phone in the hall, rushed into the kitchen to get a serviette. 'I'm sorry,' I said to her, illogically. She stroked me.

I phoned to where everyone would now be. Cousin Maurice answered. He told me she had died peacefully. Then I spoke to my mother and told her what had happened. I said I was not sure what was the right thing to do but that I felt, simply, that one was dead and we must now go to be with the one still alive. 'Go,' she said, 'you're crying.'

But on the way out, *en route*, with Tanya Joe and my eldest son, Lindsay Joe (the youngest had a party to go to and could not be persuaded to give it up, nor could we press a child of seven to measure priorities involving death), on the way we felt we must call in on Uncle Harry. Dusty entered the flat and immediately burst into tears on Thelma's shoulder. We had tea and I went in to see my dead aunt. She lay on the bed, they'd not covered her face, it was ashen, her mouth frozen open.

Over tea we talked. Thelma said, unemotionally, her tears for the moment used up: 'The last hours were awful. We couldn't do anything for her. She just gasped and gasped. But even so she wanted us to help her get up and sit in the armchair.' Norma said: 'We had a problem with the bedpan. She felt she wanted to do something and so we got her on to it but she couldn't do anything.'

'So I said', continued Thelma, 'I said, "Do you want us to leave it there?" "Leave it," she said. "It isn't uncomfortable?" I asked. "I've had worse," she said and she laughed.' We all laughed.

It was a fast drive to Norwich. We made straight for the

hospital and by chance found Mother Bicker and her daughter-in-law, Cissie, outside. 'Well, he's a changed man from yesterday,' said Mother Bicker. 'Yesterday I wouldn't know him but he's king today, king, my dear. 'Course, don't you go in 'specting to see him as you knew him.' At which she broke down but for no more than seconds. A firm woman, portly, and determined to hold everything (including her own sanity) together, she never allowed herself more than a brief 'pipe of the eye', like a safety valve.

We went into the ward. He was not as bad as we'd expected but as soon as he saw Dusty he began to weep and Dusty wept with him. He simply looked confused and offended as though betrayed by those to whom he'd given a trust that was absolute. His face, sunken and gummy without the prop of false teeth, emphasized his air of baby-like dependence; his grey hair, cropped and upright like Stan Laurel's, edged his bewilderment with madness. But madness, bewilderment, babyness or not, he was very much alive and more so than we had anticipated.

We told him how relieved we were to find him in such good form. He was at pains to tell us how well he'd eaten and how he himself could see the change for the better. We urged him to keep his spirits up because all the signs *were* so encouraging. 'Good thing,' he said, 'thaas a good thing, then, 'cos I don't wanna stay in longer'n I hev to.'

The children came in and he wept anew on seeing them. They looked at him in amazement, unused yet to the world going wrong; but fortunately their fund of natural comfort avoided adding awkwardness to the moment.

There were three other men in the ward who all assured us how much better he was from the night before. Poppy Bicker didn't know he'd had a stroke. He thought he was suffering from the after-effects of the operation so he was urging everyone not to have it and swearing he'd never get back into the hospital, not for anything. He was also slightly dopy from drugs. 'Thaas Paddy', he said of one of the patients. 'Thaas Paddy that is, my friend and he look after me and when I get better I'll look after him.' 'Don't you worry about me,' said Paddy who was waiting for his operation on both hips. 'You tend to yourself first.' At which Poppy cried again, saying, 'Thaas right, yes, I will, that I will, that I will.' We left him for a brief while to have lunch.

When we returned, Dusty's sister, Joy, and her husband, Charlie Keeble, were outside in the grounds. We all went into the ward and I found a doctor to speak with about Poppy's prospects and was told they were genuinely hopeful. Apparently they didn't yet know what had caused the stroke and were waiting for forty-eight hours to pass to see if he'd have another. If he could survive that time he'd be all right.

I told Poppy how pleased 'they' (the doctors) were with his recovery as though in getting well he was behaving well. His own relief was full of the humble worker's gratitude to have been made well by 'them'. The old farm labourer might not have believed *us* but to be told that those in charge felt he'd be all right was really reassuring. Then he said to Dusty: 'Go you back to the shed at Beck Farm and get you some sacks and take home some tatties and peas from the garden. We set some aside for you, look.' At which he wept again. My eldest son's amazement suddenly found voice. 'What an extraordinary family this is! It's so close. And we've got so much spirit. I mean Aunty Ray's body is in one room and you cry and laugh in the other room. And Poppy lying here paralysed and crying and talking of the garden and the "tatties" he's put aside for you!'

There was little more we could do. The nurse said perhaps we shouldn't tire him further and so we drove back to Beck Farm, Redenhall, for tea. There, Mother Bicker loaded us with fresh spuds, peas and onions from their large garden. Then we went to Cissie's house for a few moments, where Dusty regretted missing her brother who was working overtime bringing in the sugarbeet; and then on for another cup of tea to sister Joy's place. Dusty had thought she might have to stay the night but now there seemed no point. There'd be no card games this trip: (sevens mainly, pontoon and whist sometimes). We could return for Aunty Ray's funeral. If necessary we could come back to Redenhall at a moment's notice. But there was no need.

We buried Aunty Ray. Poppy Bicker survived. And he fought to survive. They gave him exercises to do, such as taking a duster to polish the doors, round and round and round, moving his arms up and down and across, endlessly shining what shone, in order to keep his body fit and deserving of the life he cherished and wept for so easily. It was Mother Bicker who now took the strain, washing him down and attending to the interminable little nags the sick have need of. And in between doing that, and the normal routine of domesticity, she shopped and cleaned for her own very aged mother, the only great-grandmother my children could boast of – Granny Loombe.

One day, during a week-end visit to see how Poppy Bicker was getting on, we visited Granny Loombe. She sat listening to the news we thought would engage her, her face lined with Audenesque creases, her stubborn Bicker lips puckering back and forth in habitual defiance, and – this sent a cold shiver through me – her legs crossed with the top one, from knee-cap to foot, bouncing up and down as though in perpetual rhythm to silently sung melodies, just like her grand-daughter. It was not the inherited habit that was extraordinary but that habits could be *so* inherited; *that*, the handing on, no – the passing on – *that* was extraordinary.

Then one day Dusty went to Norfolk and collected her father, who stayed with us for a week in London, where he spent most of his time tending to our neglected garden: pruning, burning, turning the earth, scraping out the weeds from cracks between the York stone path, and playing cricket with the children. One arm was firm enough to grip while the other, the paralysed one, could just guide the bat. He was so happy that he asked to stay with us longer and we took him to our cottage in Wales in the Black Mountains, to hills and a wild landscape he'd never before seen in his life. And there, again, he helped to clean up the garden and dig fresh life into the heavy clay soil. He was full of advice and soft gaiety and found his memory sharpening so that we heard stories about events which even he'd long ago forgotten. We gathered the horses' shit from the fields to lay on the compost heap and swept up dead leaves to lay on top for the manure which would eat its way through. He sawed old timber with me and axed, with his left hand, the blocks into splinters for the fire. And he spent long hours in silence looking at this miraculous valley of rock and fern and tree and lush field that lay in front of the house, and at the scarred and creviced mountain called Lord Hereford's Knob that lay to the left of the house; staring at it all with wet old eyes as though he'd only just been born, damp and curious, into the world.

Once he asked me: 'Would you give me a bath and wash me poor ole hair please?' I undressed him and washed him down with a flannel, showering and massaging his 'poor ole hair' with shampoo. It reminded me of the days I used to wash my own father's paralysed body. But he had been incontinent whereas Poppy Bicker smelt sweet. Somehow, old men make mothers of us.

When he returned home to Norfolk, Dusty's sister, Joy, wrote: 'He's a changed man, that's for sure. Do you know what – he've started to ride a bike again.'

1972

# THE MAN WHO BECAME AFRAID

Sheridan Brewster had a moderately interesting background. His father had been an engineer in the army, stationed in India, and had been confronted by retirement at the same time India confronted independence. He'd stayed, hired himself to the provincial government of Mysore and sent his son back to England to study aerodynamics, in which father Brewster with good sense saw the future.

Each year Sheridan returned to India for the summer holidays and for two years all went well. In the third year Mr Brewster senior contracted a malarial disease which left both him and his fortunes depleted. It was not total disaster, but it meant he could not afford to pay for his son's summer trip. Sheridan, an accommodating and resourceful young man, decided to hitch-hike. He and a friend took to the road, discovered themselves, and stayed on it four years.

For Sheridan Brewster it was four years of building another personality. New rhythms and attitudes to life shattered his comfortable little routines of study and his friendly dogmas about decency. He made contact with suffering, a contact which gave him a completely different perspective on the words he'd heard used to describe it: one nodded sadly at mere words, but faced with the actual experience of suffering one's very body seemed to undergo transformation – shivering, nausea, angry tension.

Most to affect him, though, had been the encounters with

groups of guerrillas in Africa, for whom he and his friend engaged in some gun-running, partly as a means of earning a living, but mainly to answer their newly awakened sense of outrage. It was not an intimate or lengthy involvement, but close and long enough for them to turn from revolutionary exhilaration to dis-enchantment with the internal quarrels of the rivalling brotherly Left under pressure. A sad disillusionment.

They moved on, depressed. (Or rather Sheridan's friend moved on – to a life of bohemian wandering which, merging with the lives of the next generation of travellers, became known as hippy wandering, though by then he was middle-aged and a bit pathetic; not because it's pathetic to be found still wandering in middle-age but because he himself no longer enjoyed it.) Sheridan, on the other hand, determined to take up his studies again, but now in the less demanding though possibly duller region of heating and ventilating.

This was in 1950 and he was twenty-five. In the twenty-five years that followed he went through left-wing student politics; an idealistic partnership in a firm of heating consultants, which he tried to run as a co-operative dealing exclusively with emerging African states, but which failed due to the greed of his partners and the corruption of certain ministers in the new bureaucracies; then into consultancy with an American firm which took him to the States where affluence worked its – not inevitable but fairly reliable – corrosive spells, and where, finally, he met a patrician New England lady called Mildred, whom he wedded. It was a mistake.

Sheridan and his wife were, as she suggested at the end of their very first year, 'out of sync'. But just as it's possible to watch, understand and make allowances in a home-movie, for the words following just a little too late upon the actions, so they tolerated, but kept missing, the point of one another.

Mildred Harding's tallness had had dignity when youth had

given her confidence, but complaint and twenty-five years of ageing in a foreign country had bent the willowy Yankee maiden till she came physically to resemble her lanky father, whose intellect, instead, she'd have preferred and Sheridan had thought she possessed. He'd been a brilliant lawyer who, too intelligent to pretend about everything, developed a biting tongue that made him more feared than successful, and who, though he'd ended up seedy and cynical, deserved a daughter to have adored, cared for and spoilt him. Instead Mildred grew up spoilt *by* him for her wit and beauty which, Sheridan soon realized, were somewhat spurious, producing an arrogance unmerited by a talent for *anything*, neither lasting long anyhow, and both bloated by the forced feeding of her father's irresponsible adoration. It was not a blessed marriage.

During that last quarter century the world moved through McCarthy, Hungary, Suez, the so-called 'angry' writers, the semination of the E.E.C., the rise of De Gaulle, Aldermaston, Committee of 100, civil disobedience, the Cuban revolution – whose long-haired youthful leaders encouraged the cult of youth and long hair and revolution – civil rights marches in the States, the assassination of John F. Kennedy, the insane cruelties of the Vietnam conflict, the Chinese Cultural Revolution and the spread of Maoism in the West, Black Panthers, Weathermen, the Israeli/Arab six-day war, Biafra, the assassination of Robert Kennedy, the Russian occupation of Prague, the Paris student demonstrations, the murder of Martin Luther King, Middle-East hi-jackings, the first landing on the moon, Northern Ireland, Black September assassinations, the Angry Brigade, Bangladesh ...

Sheridan, like many, was catastrophe-dazed and spiritually pock-marked by the endless repetition of oppression, ill-conceived and doomed defiance, and the brutal suppression by a cynical establishment of that defiance. He understood the cynicism and the defiance and settled down to an uncomfortable and

increasingly melancholy life with both in the protective bosom
of his local Greenwich Labour Party and the, by now, rejecting
bosom of a wife whose weary astringency had once excited him
to marriage.

And then ... the tumbling, tumbling ...


PART ONE
It began as a joke, moved on into discoveries, and then came the
signs.

First the joke: 'Me?' Sheridan would say, 'I'm frightened of
everything. What, not be frightened? In this world? Every
minute?'

But he said it with charm and panache so that one didn't think
he could *ever* be afraid of anything. On the contrary, he exuded
the air of a man to whom one would trust one's life: he had the
right balance of calm and healthy fear. 'Frightened of everything!'
he'd say in a tone reassuring for its mixture of confidence and
doubt. And the intellectual conceit of being both prone to fear
and able to confess it gave him a pleasure which reassured even
himself.

But words, he was to discover, containing as they do a power
born through centuries of experience, are not symbols to be used
carelessly; they may have a slow fuse of meaning which smoulders
for a long time but they finally explode into blinding truths.
There is the story of the young Russian poet who declared he
would one day kill himself, which at once attracted an outraged
warning from an older writer: 'Don't ever say such a thing,
never! Call yourself a poet? Don't you understand the power of
words? Say something like that to yourself just once, only once,
and such is the hypnotic power of a word's meaning, such is the
compulsion of a spoken vow that even if you've changed your
mind and don't want to die you'll be driven to it.'

Then came the discoveries.

Not long after attaching to himself the joke about being 'frightened of everything', the first discovery took place. It was a discovery about the nature of discovery itself and happened while the firm of Brewster and Drummond – industrial heating and ventilation consultants, of which he was the managing director and chief engineer – were trying to settle the problems of ventilation in a large canning factory near Beersheva in Israel. Even going to Israel, whose feud with neighbours refusing to acknowledge its existence had gone on since the birth of the country, was an occasion for Sheridan Brewster to declare with his reassuring smile how scared he was of entering such dangerous territory.

'But,' he humbly declared, proudly paraphrasing Shakespeare, 'he who is afraid to die dies a thousand times,' and with a brave face set out for the unpromising promised land. To his surprise he found the Israelis warning him more sternly about a certain 'chumsin' (pronounced 'hum' not 'chum') than about the booby-traps of the Palestinian guerrillas of whom they spoke with affection; the chumsin was the real killer.

But what was a chumsin? He'd never heard of it and certainly wasn't experiencing it.

'A chumsin', they told him, 'is a dry desert wind which parches your throat and nostrils and clogs up the pores of your skin.'

He felt nothing. Or rather he felt a wind, but a pleasurable one, like any other except that it was warm, as you'd expect in the desert.

'How can you like it?' his Israeli hosts asked him, watching him turn his face up towards it for relief, as they sat outside cafés drinking Turkish coffee flavoured with hael seeds. He thought they were pulling his leg and answered, sighing: 'At last, a fresh breeze, at last.'

'Mad', they said, but enjoyed what they imagined to be English eccentricity. It had been no eccentricity, he'd actually felt relief to have the wind on his skin, then.

The job went well, the Israeli technicians were efficient and hospitable; a little lax perhaps about keeping appointments on time but they made up for it with an amusingly laconic sense of humour which, in this case, revolved around daily inquiries as to whether he'd felt the chumsin yet. He hadn't; rather, he was beginning to think it a national joke meaning something else. Then one day he 'phoned his wife in London. It was one of those undignified conversations where both unhappily pursued their predictable roles of nagger and liar and then despised themselves for so doing. She catechized him on his movements, feigning anxiety about his safety and the progress of the installation, and he replied with thinly eager warmth, pretending she did *not* want to ferret out another 'little foreign affair' until both felt able to acknowledge truthfully what each was doing, and he said, tartly: 'The release of sexual tensions while abroad is to be viewed as an inevitable custom of travel, like the need to eat raw fish in Japan or snails in Paris. Something to bear with politely, without too much fuss, as the price of international trade.'

His wife, of course, suffering from old-fashioned bonds and responses, could neither share nor enjoy his humour, and deflated, as she always did, the proud equanimity he earned for his skills and good-natured reliability among overseas clients. She scraped the shrill bottom of her salt-barrel of wit: 'Are they black-eyed?' she retaliated. 'The wives I mean. Is it like the photographs we see, streets filled with exotic girls in uniform? I hope they're not tiring you, the Israeli contractors I mean, not the wives. Hard working little lot they are – the contractors I mean.'

Sheridan was laying back on his hotel bed wretched and perspiring – not too much, he didn't do that – and wishing he'd married someone more subtle, when he felt it. The chumsin. It *was* a dry wind. How strange. The breeze that came through his window was as gentle as before, but no longer cooling. How could that be? It was the same wind as yesterday and the day before, and on those days he'd felt it refreshing. But now? It didn't make sense. That same wind was choking and unpleasant. This was his discovery: his skin, an immediate reactor you'd think, was belatedly learning the truth of what it was experiencing. Or perhaps his skin had always known but the message it sent of discomfort had not reached his brain, or his brain had ignored them, or not understood them.

He reflected on the nature of discovery: had one to be prepared for the truth, made ready to receive it, groomed in some way? He could have visited Israel and, had no one told him such a thing as a chumsin existed, he'd not have felt it. Or would he? Wasn't he denying the edifying value of experience itself? He'd thought himself a man less cluttered with preconceptions than most. Had he really needed to be told and told and told again? Surely in time he'd have come to detect the difference between the cool refreshing English breeze and a claustrophobic desert one? The discovery startled him. He was confused.

Later that year another job took him to Munich where, the locals insisted, depression set in on certain sunny days and the city's inhabitants prayed for rain. Something to do with a wind coming down off the mountains from the south, a 'foehn' they called it. Once again he didn't believe them. Whoever prayed for sunny days to go away? Until one evening, waiting in his hotel to be picked up by the Munich industrialist for whom his firm was installing a particularly complex system, the bell-boy swung into the coffee lounge calling his name and handed him a telegram. It all happened very quickly.

He was sitting in a deep, bright-red leather armchair, frowning over a problem to do with a section that had broken down and been replaced with the wrong spare part by some idiot in the London store room – when suddenly he felt as though either he'd

pulled his tie too tightly round his neck or he'd been holding his
breath too long in concentration. But whatever, he wrenched
open his collar and broke off a button. At the same moment he
heard his name called, was irritated to hear himself addressed as
Sheridan Brewster instead of the more formal Mr or Herr
Brewster (the Sheridan had always embarrassed him) and was
seconds later staring at a telegram which, designed to stir
guilts, read: IGNORE COMPLAINTS STOP I TRUST REVERE
ADORE DEPEND AND FORGIVE STOP FORGIVE. It was signed by
his wife.

Instantly melancholy, he folded the canny telegram neatly in
his steady hand to hide the wretchedness in his unsteady heart,
saw a flash of lightning through the glass front of the hotel, heard
the thunder, saw the rain come blasting down and then, from a
car, appear his German host friendly and smiling and armed with
an umbrella.

'Aren't you frightened of lightning?' his host asked.

'Me?' he replied, relieved for the opportunity to impress his
calm. 'Me? I'm afraid of everything!'

The two men smiled at the joke, shook hands and went into the
waiting vehicle where a beautiful wife offered her hand and proceeded to delight him with the programme they'd prepared for
their evening together.

'Perhaps you don't need a tie,' she said, tactfully handling the
broken-button situation, 'but I'm sure you'd like me to sew on a
replacement and fortunately I'm that kind of tedious girl-guide
lady who carries needle and cotton around for just such emer-
gencies.'

Said Sheridan's host: 'My wife is prepared, always, for everything and anything', at which thin wit they all laughed gaily.

'Thank God!' said the wife, 'for the rain.'

There! It had happened again. He'd been in the city a month
and only now realized a depression had been gathering around

him. They were unnerving, these discoveries, and put him on guard, alert, as though suddenly he'd found himself doomed to the constant company of an unpredictable stranger.

Next came the signs.

He was returning on a jet from Montreal when, about twenty minutes after take-off, the large Boeing 707 dived some few hundred feet, abruptly and without warning, causing his heart to miss a beat and his glass of wine to rise like a geyser in front of him, spilling over his suit. Whenever he became a little anxious in an aeroplane, which was rarely, for he loved flying, he looked immediately at the face of an air hostess to detect the slightest change in her composure. On this occasion he looked round sharply.

Strangely there seemed no undue panic – no air hostess had gone pale. And yet it was certainly no ordinary air-pocket bump, though it seemed that that was just what the other passengers *had* thought. Except one man, behind him, who'd obviously caught his worried glance.

'Yes,' he said, 'I felt it also, you weren't imagining things. But I'm beginning to get used to it. Hardly ever take a plane journey without something going wrong.'

And he went on to relate a list of incredible minor accidents encountered on his aeroplane flights around the world.

'I was once staring out of my window when suddenly I saw the engine catch fire. That was a quick landing I can tell you.'

By this time the captain's frighteningly calm voice was apologizing through the speakers. He had discovered a fault in the air-pressure forcing him to take quick action and lose height immediately.

'I'm sorry ladies and gentlemen if the slightly heavier than usual bump caused you any discomfort but there was no time to warn you. I'm afraid this means we'll have to return to Montreal which I'm in contact with at this moment. As soon as I've received instructions I'll be in communication with you again. The crew will be happy to ... '

Sheridan turned to the Jonah behind him who nodded a 'there-I-told-you-so' smile, and added: 'But I like their voices. Very reassuring. Mad, actually, 'cos you never know who's on board. There may be someone dashing for a life-or-death meeting – a relative may be dying; or an urgent business conference – his firm'll go under if he misses it; or a lover's rendezvous. Air pressure goes? Bang! Too bad. Back we go. And you'll see, we'll have to circle round for hours before we can land because we're too heavy with fuel and it's got to be dumped over the sea. Waste, pollution, delay, heart-break – all because a little mechanism in a huge human carrier has gone wrong. Lovely! Ironic! I love it! Fate's fancies – huh! Bloody funny.'

His laugh was irritatingly malicious. Sheridan didn't enjoy the sardonic temperament, a civilized form of small evil he thought it to be.

'Me', continued the man, 'I'm so used to it I never make absolute arrangements. Always warn the other end that something might go wrong.' He laughed ridiculously. 'Do you think that preparing for catastrophe invites it?'

Sheridan didn't think so. 'I'm disinclined to make harsh realities cosier with bits and pieces of mystic explanation', he said, with too much pomposity, which as he at once noticed and regretted it, plunged him into melancholy.

'Hm!' said the cheerful Jonah. 'Is that so?'

And neither spoke to the other from then on.

The plane wasn't given permission to land in Montreal and had to fly back to New York instead, where another aircraft belonging to the same company was able to take on the extra passengers. Sheridan rang his wife from New York to explain what was happening and became very irritated when she so obviously didn't believe him.

His irritation stayed with him in the plane. And as he sat waiting for take-off it turned to unhappiness tinged with self-pity which, by the time the engines started, had become fear.

Taking off from New York he experienced a trepidation that was an entirely novel emotion for him. A hitherto unknown area of his sensibility was exposed and he felt flow through it sensations he'd not known before. His stomach turned with the upwards sweep of the plane as it took off and with the awareness of the space that grew between the plane and the earth. He sensed the aircraft's enormous weight from the vibrations of the engines, whose energetic thrusting betrayed the effort needed to move so many men in their powerful metallic things. He saw the machine as being seated upon a board, which at any moment could be kicked from under them, and suddenly he began to contemplate the sensation of falling through space. There came to his memory a photograph he'd once seen of two bodies still strapped to the aeroplane seat, which had been jettisoned from the main fuselage and hurled through the air, and which had been washed ashore long after the inexplicable explosion had taken place 32,000 feet up. Had those protectively trapped passengers been conscious at the moment their seats were ejected? Had they felt themselves plunging and cursed that they'd been trapped? How many seconds does one remain conscious between knowing a plane is doomed and reaching that doom? All these and many more thoughts flickered through him with brief vividness in the few seconds of take-off, and a tiny shiver, the first of its kind he'd ever experienced, shuddered through him.

But none of this lasted long. Old reserves of self-control and confidence flooded back and soon he was enjoying the miracle of flying, as he'd always done. In fact he had forgotten all about aerophobia until one day, as his plane was landing from a business trip to Paris, the captain announced: 'No doubt you'll all have heard a little bang in the course of the flight over, this was due to

the failure of one of our three engines, which we had to shut down.
I'm sorry if any of you felt …'

Sheridan, carrying his thin sliver of a case, the metal kind,
which made him feel he was in possession of a sub-machine-gun
rather than an overnight kit, was torn between a renewal of the
fear of flying and admiration for the fact that everything had
gone well despite an engine packing up. After all, the plane had
continued its scheduled flight, and no one noticed the bang. They
were not even late. He looked at the other passengers walking
their long walks down the bleak corridors to passport control,
but saw no sign that they'd thought they'd been near to death,
and heard no animated chatter about the incident. Everything is
so fragile, he thought to himself, and then he did something he'd
never done before – he smiled at the passport control officer. The
officer snapped his passport closed, nodded, said a polite but
emotionless, 'thank you, sir,' and did not return the smile. Sheridan
sensed he'd been ingratiating and became angry with his un-
forgivably sweet and sentimental lapse.

All at once he felt tired and wanted nothing other than to
return home and sleep. But at home he fell into the routine as
before: listened affectionately to his twin daughters, aged fifteen,
playing a duet for piano and guitar, watched the news on T.V.
and a Nationwide programme of local affairs, turned to his study
and the problems of a new job which lay stretched on his drawing
board and only then, after an hour's work to appease his puritan
guilts about endeavour, did he give in and go to bed.

But bed was a battleground no less mined than the poor,
nagged and menaced world outside. With no hope of response
he stretched a starved hand out for contact with his wife's skin.
It tensed at once, like the string of an instrument tightened by an
untrained fist, and his fingers slid meekly back to between his
curled-up legs. They lay back-to-back, each reaching as far as
they could to their edges of the bed to show how absolutely they

could do without one another.

'It seems so long ago,' he said with needless whispering, 'that I've forgotten what it was about me could possibly have attracted you.'

She didn't reply for a long time. He knew she was finding it difficult to bring herself to bother.

'You were a damned, cool Englishman,' she replied with weary scorn, 'a rare catch, didn't you know?'

'Not my romantic past? Gun-running for African guerrillas and all that?'

'I never believed it.'

'It was true all the same.'

'Didn't last long though, did it?'

'Long enough,' he reflected sadly. His sadness warmed nothing in her. She breathed noisily. It made him think she must be asleep, but after a silence she added: ' ... long enough ... long enough ... to have credentials ... for public viewing ... every now and then ... when needed ... '

She was effective, could hurt, no doubt about that. He waited for the smart to subside.

'You!' he said, 'what do *you* care about anything? Cool Englishman! Huh! You fell for me because you flirted with politics as you flirted with everything!'

'Oh go to sleep, Sheridan,' she groaned, with very real boredom.

And the strange thing is – he did. Unhappiness and fear are exhausting emotions to bear.


PART TWO

It was a good sleep, refreshing. Indeed most of his nights were good in the next years during which time his practice thrived and there was a General Election, for the winning of which by the

Labour Party he gave a handsome cheque, but it didn't. The failure of his party to win came as no surprise to him and, though many things worried him, of course! he began to muse about how very little shocked him, as if old habits of survival were determined to resist the erosions of matrimony and a self-immolating world.

So, he maintained an external manner of bluff modesty, continued to pretend that nothing frightened him, by saying that everything did, while his hair greyed at a normal and attractive pace, giving his tall body and long face with its whiskery eyebrows the final distinguished touch his undistinguished life needed – like a handsome Italian filmstar making a comeback. But there were differences, in little ways to begin with, 'old-womanish', his wife called them.

The first thing she remembered (because it was only in retrospect that she understood the nature of the changes taking place) was when, one evening, after hearing on the news a gruesomely detailed story about a house burning down and killing a family of five children, Sheridan observed: '*We've* got no fire appliances, have we?'

She didn't even bother to reply. Who had? Very few of their friends, certainly. But within the week he'd bought two rope ladders, the ends of which he pronged with U-shaped staples to the floor near the window of rooms in the front and rear of the house, then neatly rolled and bundled them out of sight; and arranged for three fire extinguishers to be fitted in spots whose strategic value they quarrelled about for days.

Some weeks later, again as a result of a gory T.V. advert, showing a crippled boy with cut face talking about how in a car crash he'd been thrown through the front window, Sheridan insisted that everyone who sat in the front seat of the car should use the safety-belt. All very sensible so far, his wife had thought. But then, in the same week as the T.V. advert, he read out, one morning, from the newspaper, a report about medical research into 'flu

that had been conducted in Canada. The research team had con-
cluded that the strongest cure was prevention and the strongest
prevention was vitamin C – in great quantities.

'That's oranges and grapefruit,' he said.

'Or tablets', his wife had added, 'Redoxin.'

From which moment on he nagged her constantly to keep the
house full of citrus fruit and effervescent tablets which he forced
upon the children until they became addicts, or nearly.

His wife oscillated between cautious delight and mild irritation. On one occasion she even found herself indulging in the
warm and long-forgotten glow of real concern when he announced that he was going to spend £50 at one of those clinics
where they made tests of every part of your body. Was he sick?
A mortal illness? Something he'd kept hidden for years? No. He
wanted his blood tested for leukaemia and cholesterol contents,
his heart for cardiac imperfections, his lungs for cancer, his brain
for tumours and his everywhere for everything. All results were
negative.

As time passed he looked less and less for work abroad, and for
the work abroad that could not be turned down he sent out other
partners. He even once turned down a job in Tunisia, because he
feared he might let slip in conversation that he'd done business
with Israel, and would perhaps be assaulted. There was no logic
in this train of thought and he felt very ashamed afterwards since,
apart from not enjoying the humiliating sensation of cowardice,
he recognized how insulting it was towards his hosts. But it had
been what he'd thought of at the time as an intuition, though, he
realized afterwards, a very convenient one. He'd simply been
afraid.

His wife was confused. True, they'd mellowed a lot, but
suddenly Sheridan was around more often. She watched him
sceptically at first, imagining that his reluctance to travel was an
aberration; then scathingly, heaping upon him the rich variety of

mocking tongues she'd mustered into her emotional armoury during the long haul through the ruins of the wrong marriage; then curiously, asking him was he well or had something happened to the business; then, her natural precautions satisfied, tenderly – making special efforts to cook for him dishes he'd spoken about after a trip abroad, and buying the odd little present which she 'just happened to see and thought you'd like'.

But if Mildred found it confusing, Sheridan found it curious rather than distressing. He certainly didn't look at himself in the mirror and say, 'Sheridan, you're going to pieces. Take control!' Yet there was no denying the metamorphosis: he was shifting responsibility, he'd never done that before. His poor, bewildered wife, in her bewilderment, at once misinterpreted the process, seeing all his new actions as a sign that his feelings towards her were changing: he wanted to be nearer her for longer periods, she thought.

It was this misunderstanding had helped release those feelings of tenderness in her and her attitude towards him slowly, slowly changed from carping despite to regard. One morning this brittle New England lady confronted her husband at breakfast and, with recharged warmth, suggested he take the day off to visit an art gallery with her. Her instinct was right, sweet and eager in fact, but she'd chosen the wrong destination for its drive: he disliked art galleries. He'd had to attend many openings in the company of business acquaintances and always felt uncomfortable with the mixture of bogus admiration for what was patently not liked or comprehended, and of speculation, which was why most of the businessmen had gone. He reminded his wife of this but for once she was prepared to urge patiently. It was not the *opening* of an exhibition, it had been open for some time: why not give himself a break and come with her? Wasn't morning truancy delicious? He agreed.

The gallery was empty. No, not quite, there was a downstairs which they'd not noticed and coming up was a stout little man with glasses, about sixty years old, and a young man, also small and also with glasses, who was obviously the gallery-owner.

'I don't want guarantees,' the older man was saying, 'you can't give them, I know. But your word. Give me that.'

The young man smiled the seductive smile of self-deprecation, lifted his arms wide and shrugged. The older one accepted the gesture and continued: 'I'll be frank. You can make a fool of me. Sell me a piece of land and I know what I'm buying, but a canvas? In the art world I know nothing from nothing. I like things, yes, and them I'll buy because I like them and I don't care what I pay. But an investment is a different thing altogether. I was sent here because they told me you make painters. It sounds mad to me but that's what they say. *You* sell a painter and he's got a value. I don't know how you do it and I don't care, I just have a sum of money I want to put into paintings. It appeals to me – you can hang your money on the walls and it not only looks spiritual instead of material, like money looks, but it grows in value also, which money doesn't. That really does appeal to me.'

'You *are* frank,' the young man said. 'I like that.'

'It doesn't matter to me if you like it or you don't like it – I *am*. Now, what's good?'

'Then I'll be frank with you. I don't know!' The young gallery-owner this time shrugged a variation of his first shrug – no raised arms, and smiled a variation of his first smile – no self-deprecation. The joke, he hoped, would achieve the intimacy that didn't exist.

'Look at this man,' he pointed to the artist's paintings which were on exhibition, 'why is he bought? Ask him what interests him and he says "water". Water and its effects on objects, its movement, its "distorting properties". And what does he paint? Swimming pools in rich houses, exotic fish in expensive aquariums on expensive sideboards, people taking a bath in the latest see-through plastic tub, multi-coloured tiled cabinets with showers coming from all sides. Water! But in affluent settings. And affluent people buy them, not because they love his handling of wetness, but because it reminds them of their own homes, it echoes their tastes which they imagine are good. But now look what he's done.'

They paused to give greater attention to what the little fat man had been constantly looking at over these last days: photographs of trees, alongside which had been drawn in ink, minutely reproduced and tinted with moss greens, silver and burnt browns, sketches of the same trees.

'Forests!' spat out the young entrepreneur. 'Who'll buy them?'

'Seems to me they're nearly all sold,' observed the older man drily.

'Then they shouldn't have been! I mean it's not what was expected and it's not why his first exhibition sold out. How many people own forests? And now he's tempting fate. Look at them. He's got the world's best photographer to photograph nature's trees and then he's gone into competition with both of them: the photographer and nature, as if daring the onlooker to make a choice between the real thing and his reproduction of it. Isn't that mad? What's better than nature herself? But he's challenged her! And has he succeeded? Who knows! Defiance! Why should anyone buy him? Such arrogance.'

Sheridan and Mildred, unnoticed, listened to all this, cheating a bit as they stayed hidden round a corner in the gallery. Its effect upon them both was shattering. But for very different reasons. Mildred was appalled to hear art actually spoken about as an investment! She'd known of the process, of course, but somehow hearing painting discussed in these terms was altogether different, and she expressed her disgust to Sheridan, who now enjoyed the scathing whip of her tongue since it scarred skins other than his. 'Wasn't that a performance? Wasn't he the cutest cunningest

dealer ever? The right mixture of critical jargon and bogus bewilderment – enough of the one to impress his knowledge and of
the other to impress his honesty. Not that he sounded as though
he could go much further with either even if given the chance.'

For Sheridan it was not a question of moral outrage – he'd
always known about speculation in the art world. No, on the
contrary, with a mixture of distaste and exhilaration, he found
himself wondering why he'd not himself ever bought the works
of painters about whom he too had had hunches. After all no man
could be expected to want to remain in the business of heating
and ventilation forever. Travel had lost its thrill; he was tired of
expending energy on new relationships and having opinions on
everything over too many lunches. The problems of installation
were increasing; standards in skills had lowered and he didn't
want to be bothered to apologize to the clients or keep tele-
phoning transport firms, or shout at indifferent workmen or
humour their threats; they were right! What did it matter if
craftsmanship was low, that wasn't the point – even if it were
high they'd never earn what he earned out of the business. He
couldn't be bothered to find arguments countering such attitudes,
he just couldn't. His heart had gone out of it all.

What, therefore, of the future? Shouldn't he be buying things
which would increase in value? The cost of living was rising, industrial unrest could produce chaos, and looming over everything
was entry into Europe with its increasing competition and all the
attendant heartache. The girls would need funds to keep them
while at university, where would it all come from? He'd seen
money go, he knew its deceptive ways; it was the most expensive
commodity to buy. And he'd watched men grow old and pathetic
because their dignity had been based on the high standards which,
in retirement, they'd not been able to sustain.

It was a curious sensation, this anxiety for the future. He'd not
felt it before. Not that he was now in a panic. The anxiety was

not acute. His pondering upon the days ahead was more contemplative than frenetic, and at that moment he would have denied any connection whatsoever between his enquiry about prices of the few remaining pictures in the gallery and his concern for the future. In fact as they casually moved before the canvases his words to his wife were: 'Wouldn't it be amusing to buy some paintings over, say, a year, or some "objects", and then check what their value is a year later? See if we've been right and what the percentage of the increase is alongside, for example, the interest on a building society?'

'You mean', said Mildred, 'play bingo with art?'

But he rose above her sarcasm – and easily persuaded her to do the same, for her tongue was losing its taste for stinging – and together they spent many very happy afternoons over the next three months looking in expensive antique shops and galleries and, something they'd not done before, it being the kind of thing one promised oneself but never actually did, attending sales. They filled their house with old prints, Victorian watercolours, art-nouveau fruit bowls, the canvases and sculpture of young artists whom they'd read about or heard spoken of, and they waited.

While they waited, Sheridan had an accident, painful but not drastic; he walked into a plate glass door which he didn't think was there and broke his nose. Actually it gave him a rest, though he never admitted to it being such. For three weeks he was relieved of the need to be responsible and he guiltily experienced the pleasures of inaction during which time the nature of the accidental was uppermost in his mind, and his thoughts ran: thank goodness it was not worse. What if I had been run over! How they'd have mourned. Still, they're provided for. Provided for? Yes, but how much provided for? What *am* I worth dead? Insurance! I must check on it, on all insurance in fact, contents of the house – Good God! the contents! the new contents! Of course we're under-insured!

The next day he contacted his insurance broker and told him he wanted to reassess the contents of his house. The delighted broker was only too willing but warned him he'd have to itemize the contents of each room. So that when he came out of hospital he found himself going through the rooms and giving a hard cash value to all the bits and pices of furniture he and Mildred had gathered with love – as opposed to those later acquisitions which had been gathered in speculation. As he did so he complained and raged against the immorality of insurance ethics which greedily exploited man's fear of the future, and his broker listened and agreed and was far more lucid about the iniquities of the capitalist system, the insurance part of which he was an even greater expert on than Sheridan.

Such informed and readily offered agreement slightly deflated Sheridan's sanctimony but then the broker was used to patiently handling those tortuously apologetic clients who with scruple and reluctance insured themselves up to the hilt. It was a frenzied period and Sheridan covered everything, so much so that he was worth a great deal more dead than alive.

The frenzy grew and his hoarding habits expanded. Everything seemed collectable. An appetite that was obsessive filled him. One day, at a duty dinner with the Greenwich Labour Party's chairman – an ex-water prospector – Sheridan foolishly asked whether the wine was 'a bit off'. The chairman, a murderously steely man, slowly rolled the wine around in his glass and said, simply: 'It's a Château Margaux '45.'

Sheridan blushed, apologized and told a lie about a departing cold.

The chairman insulted his confusion by ignoring it. 'In the mid-'sixties,' he said, 'I bought a case of Château Latour 1961. Cost me £35. Worth £165 now.' He sipped his Margaux '45. 'In ten years' time,' he continued, 'each bottle'll be worth £100.'

Sheridan was deeply impressed. Next day he went into an

olde-looking wine shop with bow-fronted windows and asked, as nonchalantly as he could, for Château Latour 1961. The wine merchant smiled indulgently and, knowing a novice when he saw one, sold him instead a case of the same wine from the 1960 vintage. A hotelier friend told him that, frankly, it was only mediocre, so he sold it, after a year, at a profit of 25 p the case. But the bug had bitten him. An old cellar they had never used was cleared, cleaned and racks installed. In addition to sales, they attended wine tastings and – talked around. The most unexpected people were wine collectors. The chemist on the corner, for example, who sold him three dozen Château Cos d'Estournel '62 which he later read in a wine magazine had 'passed its best'. It strained the relationship with the chemist, but he gave one case to a business associate who had been marginally helpful to him in a very spectacular way, drank another and exchanged the third for a magnum of '34 Château Margaux which he secretly found decrepit. Wine prices rocketed following the 1970 vintage and, with shame, he felt his greed grow. He bought fifty assorted cases from three different wine merchants of the less scrupulous sort but somehow he always seemed to miss the bus, getting 'worthy' '67s and missing the 'outstanding' '66s. He even had a case or two from the disastrous '68 vintage fobbed off on to him. He hummed and ha'd over the 1970 Château Trotanoy, turning it down as too dear at £3.50 the bottle. Two months later it had risen to £5 and, in a panic, he snapped up four cases. When this particular obsession had abated he was the owner of a cellar of some five hundred bottles, three-quarters of them mediocre wines from mediocre years.

The next passion to intoxicate him began when, accompanying one of his partners into a second-hand bookshop one casual lunch-time, he heard a gasp and turned to see his partner transformed. Eyes shining and face animated, he was saying: 'Good God! Good God! Poetry Chicago! Early numbers of Poetry Chicago!

Wallace Stevens! H. D.! Zukofsky! What an incredible item!'

'Incredible item' seemed an affected but seductive way to refer to an old poetry magazine – it was somehow comfortable to do so, gave one a sense of belonging, like calling wines 'worthy'. He'd never seen his colleague in such a state. The discovery had given his body a terrible drive. He seemed to clench his knees and tighten his jaw, then, realizing he might be revealing too much eagerness, he relaxed into a posture of awful cunning. Sheridan was amazed. Amazed and repulsed. Repulsed and mesmerized. A new obsession was being communicated to him.

One day, glancing at a page in *The Times* which he usually skipped through, he read about a sale of rare editions, and that clinched it. He and Mildred were sent scouring the bookshops for first printings. They had a slow start. A first edition of the Yeats collected plays, 'binding in good condition, sir, jacket still clean, Wade says there were only two thousand,' was available for £10. The 1946 little Dent edition of Dylan Thomas's *Deaths and Entrances* was offered to him at £35. Good God! 1946! A year after the war. That was a yesterday, only a yesterday! Expensive, but the fever was gripping him. Collecting poetry made him feel less shabby, so he searched for magazines, like his colleague, then confessed to himself that he didn't really understand poetry. After talking around, he took the advice to collect an author and decided on his favourite, Henry James. But second-hand dealers, sensing his innocence, artfully insinuated an awareness of the need to collect everything – not only first edition James but paperback James, periodicals containing James' articles, critical books on James' novels and – this finally turned him off – all the foreign editions of James. It was too arduous.

His colleague next put him on to the idea of collecting the elite presses – a holy quest that appealed particularly to Mildred – such as The Nonesuch Press limited editions, more expensive but fewer of them. They tried. Sheridan used to spoil himself on afternoons in which he felt wretched by entering strange second-hand bookshops. The truancy made him feel guilty, as though it were pornography he were collecting. But though he entered the shops anticipating the thrill of discovery he usually left them in shrunken disappointment. They toyed with the Kelmscott Press editions, then flirted with the modern presses like Hand & Flower Press, Fantasy Press, Fulcrum Press, Trigram Press. Lovely names. But they felt it a shabby pursuit and soon they tired. Though not before their bedroom had become cluttered with battered volumes, obscure titles, and the slim editions of once hopeful, but now forgotten, poets.

Their last madness was stamps. A feeble fluttering. One of his daughters asked him if the office ever received mail from Japan because they were doing a project on the country at school. Philately! How selfish he'd been. All those countries he'd visited and he'd not brought back stamps. So the order went out for his colleagues to bring back stamps from wherever they travelled, and he joined the Philatelic Bureau, who efficiently despatched him new British issues and their first-day covers. Grandchildren! That was his excuse.

But, as with all passions which are an illness rather than a love, it, too, dwindled and even passed. Five hundred bottles was all they ever laid down and one bedroom all they ever sacrificed to literature. And when they emerged, it was as if from a deep cavern, where little light had penetrated and where furtive animals had scurried, sneakily anxious about their sneaky neighbours, clutching snatched foods for a time of famine.

PART THREE

The man who pretended to be afraid of nothing by pretending he was afraid of everything became afraid of everything. What had stood as a proud jest now tumbled, echoing hollow through the following years of his life. The landmarks of the journey were stark.

Mildred and Sheridan had, through their hoarding escapades, been drawn closer together. As two weary fighters they'd collapsed into each other's arms. Now, like the soft mist blurring what the day contains, they entered into some lovely physical ways: he would hold her hand as they walked along streets, or lay his head in her lap while they watched a television play; sometimes, as she was in the midst of cooking, he'd gently come behind her and slip his hands to her breasts flicking kisses at her neck. It seemed like the second bloom of love, all thrilling, warm. To love she could respond, and respond she did, with gratitude. Yet, though she couldn't say what, something was wrong. It took three certain nights, and the events between, to tell her.

The first night was the night of his fiftieth birthday. They decided to celebrate it quietly with Mildred taking him out to dinner over which she presented him with his present: a gold ring with two tiny ivory doves folded into each other. He was very moved and had great difficulty holding back tears.

'Though why I should refrain from tears God alone knows,' he said. 'I read an article in a magazine the other day where nine famous and very tough men confessed to crying. There was a boxer, a wrestler and a very sardonic novelist among them.'

He gripped her hand, rather too gruffly she thought, and kissed it, rather too earnestly. But that night, full of relief the days had come in which she no longer needed to be tense with approbation, and full of love for the man about whom she was relieved, Mildred gave herself to Sheridan with abandon and took from him like a stranger. Then, as they lay in bed, on their backs, he began, as though starting their loving again, to ply his fingers up and down her thigh. She stayed his hand but he rolled over on his side, buried his head in her breasts and dug and drew his fingers deep and anxiously all over her body. She tried to hold him back, laughing a little in the hope he was simply being over-playful.

'Whoa! Such passion. In one night!'

'No, let me.' He sounded distressed rather than amorous.

'What'll you be like at sixty?' she joked. But his movements were too fierce. She had to insist he stop.

The next morning he awoke at a high pitch of irritability.

'Disorder!' he cried, 'the house is like a slum. I can find nothing, nothing!'

He was looking for boot polish in the shoe-box and after ten minutes had found it on a shelf under the stairs.

'Don't you know disorder wastes time?' he shouted at Mildred. 'Don't you know I've only got another twenty more years to live? Maybe fifteen! Ten! Why am I being made to spend precious time looking and looking and fraying my temper when I could be spending both in pleasure or producing?' Mildred tried to pacify him by asking him to list what was wrong and she'd see what she could do.

'Someone borrows my ink and never returns it.' He began with the suppressed calm of a fury which rose. 'I have to look for hours for my dressing-gown. When I want a blue shirt all the white ones are pressed, when I want a white one I can only find blue ones. And meal times! Can't I even have my meals at the right time? Can't there *always* be a supply of coffee in the house? Can't someone *else* 'phone a repair man if the T.V. breaks down? Can't my letters be left in the *same* place when I get home in the evenings? I don't want to waste my nerves. A man's only got one life. Get an au-pair. For Christ's sake get help.'

So that was it. He was starting on his campaign for an au-pair again. For years they'd been without help in the house. Mildred had sworn that when the girls had turned thirteen she'd do for evermore without au-pairs – servants in disguise! They embarrassed her. Not only that, they engaged her emotions in silly love affairs and were around on days she desperately needed to feel alone in the house. But most important: she had a great desire to know she could run the house on her own. It was a question of pride. She'd never been a woman to use intellectual needs as an excuse to avoid domesticity. She didn't deny it in others but it was not for her. An inheritance from her father, who had always been scathing about women claiming the right to abandon house in pursuit of profession and then pursuing ambition. He'd said: 'Once upon a time the division of labour was sensible – women would have the ambitious fire, their husbands would be the burners. Great team. They'd breathe hell into their old men, spur them on with an ecstatic fervour, on and ever upwards! Lovely, unblushing fervourists they were. But now? Now they want to be *on* the throne instead of the powers behind it. Mistake! Awful, awful mistake. For all of us. Temperamentally unsuited for thrones. Men must caution, women urge. It's always been known, right from the beginning of time. That's why they made stories about it. Adam and Eve and all that.'

His daughter, an 'unblushing fervourist' herself, had of course argued fervently against him, but now? Ah! now she was learning that what one argues against in youth is certain to become, even in a small degree, part of one's adult pillar of faith. Not that she'd had the luck or talent to be either the *eminence*, or its *grise*; she'd been neither a professional in her own right nor an urger-on-to greater-heights. But she did retain this perversely traditional delight in running her own home. So, no more au-pairs. And it was thus for three years.

Until now, in these dark days of Sheridan Brewster's disintegration, another feature of which was this frantic demand to everyone in the house for order. So, Mildred got on to an agency who found an au-pair girl from the Philippines, whom she went to collect at the station and discovered could not speak a word of English. Mildred controlled her anger for having allowed herself to be bullied into this situation, from which she'd sworn to escape forever, and took the girl home. As soon as the girl saw her pretty room she wept, and explained her life in a torrent of words which Mildred could not understand. Mildred comforted her, gave her a glass of wine and told her to unpack and get a good sleep. All this she did with exaggerated hand-signs and facial contortions which left her exhausted. In the morning she woke the girl and saw, to her mortification, that the major item in her small collection of worldly goods was a cooking pot!

On the first day the girl followed Mildred around the house carefully watching everything that was done. On the second day she tried Hoovering and placed the pipe in the wrong end, coating the living room with a fine and evenly distributed dust. Then she mistook the washing machine for the washing-up machine and smashed a dozen or so colourful mugs. On the evening of the second day they had a dinner party for some visiting Ugandans and Mildred showed the girl how to lay the table. She learned well, and in the morning when the family came down for breakfast they found the table beautifully laid for dinner, complete with wineglasses and an uncorked bottle of wine set in the centre.

Mildred was furious. Not in front of the girl but later when she packed her off to make the beds.

'I don't know', she said to her husband, 'whether it's because she can't speak English or because she's thick.'

'Or because *you* can't speak Spanish,' said Sheridan, a tactless thing to say and which earned him the apex of her scorn.

'Don't *you* moralize to me about the arrogance of English-speaking nations. *You* insisted on an au-pair, *you* wanted the servant and *you* insisted she should come from an "emerging" country. Well there she is. Educable but useless. Raw material. Go on. Educate her. *You* learn Spanish. *You* teach her how to be an "equal" servant. *You* enter into sophistries about us simply exchanging our wares. "You see my dear",' Mildred began her too accurate imitation of her husband, '"look at it like this: *you're* helping *us*, which is what you can do for the moment, and *we're* giving you accommodation and the chance to learn English, which is our way of helping *you*. Oh, and don't forget, this is Mildred and I'm Sheridan."'

Sheridan ignored her outburst and suggested they ring a friend who also had a Filipino au-pair but one who could speak English. She came and Mildred asked her to ascertain whether the girl could speak or understand English or whether she was simply not very bright. The interpreter spoke to the newcomer from her land and reported back with dignity in her own slow, broken English the following: 'Yes, she understand English a little, and a little she speaks also, but she dares not because she is ashamed of you both.'

The effect upon Sheridan was extreme. Though he and Mildred had both laughed, she forgot and he remembered. First sardonically, then painfully. 'She is ashamed of you both.' Hadn't enough wounds been opened up without the language, ill-used, mocking him?

They kept the girl, who of course finally settled down to become a real help and enjoy her new life in England, a country where many strangers discover the standards by which to measure misery in their own lands but lose the will to return and remedy them.

One evening, not long after the affair with the Filipino girl, Sheridan returned home from the office with a bunch of flowers for Mildred. An ordinary enough event, except that the bunch of flowers was extraordinary. It was enormous.

'You must be mad,' she said.

'But deliciously mad,' he suggested. 'Come on, admit it. Super deliciously.' He was reeling around the house looking where he could lay them. Normally on arrival a bunch of flowers can lay on a hall table or by a kitchen sink – but these?

'I went in to the shop and just couldn't stop. I said, "I'll have these, and these, and six of those and a dozen of those and some of that and some of this" – I mean, it just seemed, just suddenly seemed as though a normal bunch was so paltry. "Flowers in profusion", I said, "that's what I'll get her," I said. And I did.'

He finally dumped them on the floor. There were two hundred flowers and he'd paid nearly £50 for them.

'But what's the occasion?' she demanded to know.

'Occasion! Occasion! Who needs an occasion?'

Sheridan had always been kind. Of meanness Mildred had never to complain. But such magnificent extravagance, such colourful exuberance – she was overwhelmed, thrilled. That night, as on his fiftieth birthday, she again gave herself to Sheridan with something bordering on ecstasy, and took from him like a full and brimming boy. But again, though with more urgency, he ran hard fingers over her flesh as though wishing to scratch rivers of blood on her, and once more she was forced, with disappointment, to hold him off.

Mildred woke next day feeling real concern. Did the extremes in Sheridan's behaviour really indicate the fever prelude to a mental disintegration? She was a tough lady, disinclined either to drastic analysis or drastic remedy. Most people go to pieces for want of love or friendship she thought. So, gather his friends!

Jock Lamb, a venerable, grey-haired old stalwart of the Greenwich Labour Party, came one evening for dinner with his plain and silent wife, a single-minded woman who seemed to know she'd never understand what it was any of them ever quarrelled about, but they *did*, and she had to put up with it and sit still until it was all over, sometimes nodding asleep while the only 'real solutions' to the world's problems were hurled around her. Both of them were at ease with and adored by the Brewsters and on this evening had joined a dinner of eight including a couple from the office and visiting young German newly-weds, who were that strange mixture of aggressive socialist and business entrepreneur. Left-wing Eurocrats they're called. A discussion began about the new acquisitions in the Brewster's home.

The young couple from the office raised the first questions about the immorality of collecting them. Mildred told a half-truth: 'Who's collecting? We like them!'

But it came out guiltily as half-truths often do, irritating Sheridan, who responded casually, attempting to treat it all as a joke. The German couple, whom he knew possessed a similar collection, remained silent, which increased his irritation. Then Jock, sucking his pipe and looking defiantly at a twisting stem of art-nouveau extravaganza which slithered its silver way up the partition doors, thoughtfully made his slow observations: 'Not nice, not nice at all,' he said. 'I'd understand if you were looking for bargains. Everyone loves to think they've found something of value or beauty for nothing. But to hang what doesn't give you pleasure, to hoard and haggle about the worth of something, which in your heart you think is worthless, to substitute a quick buck for real endeavour – well!'

'But who says we think it's worthless?' Sheridan replied. 'We'll probably end up keeping it all because we like it so much. Besides', he added, contradicting himself, 'it's a game. Or you could even call it an economic study: what pays greater dividends in our rotten capitalist society – trust funds or art?'

Jock added very little more, a fact which made Sheridan even angrier since the scant response created a void in which he seemed to hear the great dullness of his hollow arguments. Actually Sheridan could take anything Jock said because his affection for him was very deep but then, as often happens with close friends, he went on to make Jock pay for the irritations caused by strangers and his own imperfections.

'Oh the Left! The bloody Left! Puritan! Colourless! Dreary! You know what we should be doing? Collecting donations for *investment*. Let the *interest* contribute to Party funds. That appeals to me that does. Make the system work for its own destruction. But no! We're always terrified of dirtying our hands. And it's silly, really. We use banking systems, we buy in shops which give other men profit, the Party itself lives off the fat incomes of wealthy sympathizers, and you, Jock, are among the worst offenders, for encouraging the outworn, dainty and bankrupt moralities of bible socialism, which make old men saintly and the rest of us powerless.'

He felt ashamed. His guilt had been transparent, his defence shabby and, into the bargain, shrill. But however irritated he felt over his moral and intellectual lapse he was even more concerned about another part of that evening's happenings. Saying good-night to his guests, he caught himself hopping around pretending it was cold, and using that as an excuse to close the front door on them instead of his normal courtesy of waiting till they were out of sight. But it was not the cold that drew him in, it was his bladder; and it was the fourth time in the last hour. What a finale to high controversy.

Noticing it made him realize the affliction was not new. And there was something else (he was almost too embarrassed to ac-knowledge it to himself, being one of that dwindling band of people who still find such bodily functions and their mention an affront): his urination had lost its force! Yes, it was funny and humiliating and absurd but it was depressingly true. Even more absurd was that he'd been like this for the last year and had not registered it. He peed frequently and feebly.

Ageing was his first explanation. He reminded himself that he was fifty. Then he thought it might simply be psychological – too much work. Then he thought it might be cancerous – had the big check-up missed something? Then he took control and told him-self not to be foolish and indulgent. But it was no good. On that evening began an obsession from which he could not break away, and which the negative results of his overhaul did not help: he

was aware of his body. For the first time in his life he was conscious of functions and movements he'd taken casually for granted.
All appeared stiff, clumsy and flabby. He noticed veins protruding
from the back of his hands; thin blue streaks behind his legs. He
wheezed when he ran, puffed when he made love. His remedy
was firm: he stopped smoking and took up morning exercises.
Mildred was impressed he stopped smoking but the sight of him
panting away at press-ups added to her growing view of him as –
she had to say it – pathetic, heartless though the word.

But the tumbling, for that's what it was, an inexorable slither-
ing downhill, punctuated by feeble attempts to push himself up,
the tumbling, tumbling didn't stop. And he noticed that it didn't.
Not every diagnosis is helpful. 'Locate the problem and it's nine-
tenths of the solution,' had at one time made perfect sense to him.
Not so now. What if the problem has no solution, or no solution
*you* can muster, or no solution you can muster in time? All you
then locate is the inevitability of disaster, the locating of which
hastens it. It was like what they called in the current jargon of the
new science of futurology an 'exponential growth' rather than a
'linear' one. One fear revealed two others, making three; each of
the three exposed two more, making nine; the nine flaws then
unearthed eighteen more, making one hundred and seventy-one,
and so on. More or less. He'd been reading about the exponential
growth of population and wealth and how it would produce a
great gap between those who had and those who had not, and
how resources would be diminishing at the same rate. A frightening picture, the more so since it was beyond his control. So that he
had a language handy to describe his disintegration. Oh yes, he
thought, they not only provide me with the neurosis but also with
the words that really bring its awfulness home to me. Thank you.
Thus the tumbling was given momentum for being so painfully
apparent.

How could he stop such awful decline in which, by now, both

fear and self-disgust were feeding off each other? There seemed no reasonable answer. He *was* growing old. Pleasure *had* gone, irretrievably, from his work. Fervour *had* evaporated from his political beliefs, and curiosity no longer drove him into relationships with people. It seemed to him he understood the state in which men take their lives: not for hatred of life itself but for the incontrovertible fact of their own scant calibre for which *they can see* no remedy; of their own self-doubting for which *they* know no answer; of that awareness which each man possesses of and for himself and cannot articulate, and which no one, no one, no one else can explain away.

It seemed to him he understood that state though it was not yet the one into which he had fallen. Some defiance was left. Previously he'd bought flowers. Fifty pounds worth! A shameful act, he'd thought, in that it pretended to an extravagant nature not really belonging to him; the glamour was rooted in his privilege rather than his personality. Which realization drove him not further away from such similar acts but deeper into them, in the belief that a really wild act of extravagance would prove possession of a brave and careless nature, a true indifference to the misfortunes of an indifferent life. One day, taking the only stocks he'd ever dared to buy – £1,000 worth of British Transport at 4½ per cent, a nationalized industry! – he cashed them before maturity and, with £550 bought, outright, an almost new but comparatively cheap Sprite sports car. Knowing she'd always wanted a fast car to herself he presented it to Mildred.

Her responses were conflicting. Initially she was delighted. She gasped, sat on the edge of the front wall to the house and just stared. The chord struck in her seemed grandiloquent, but as the notes disentangled themselves from the echo, she realized there was no harmony. Everything was out of key. She was the wrong age. He was the wrong person to have bought it for her. It wasn't even the model she'd wanted. He'd not consulted her. In fact it hardly seemed purchased for her pleasure. But his eyes showed such expectancy of her pleasure, there was so much openness in his face that she could not disappoint him, and gave him the satisfaction of the gratitude he seemed to want.

And for a third time, that night, she discovered reserves of passion in them both that should have left them sweetly exhausted. Passion and sweetness there was, to begin with, but they turned to distress. At a certain moment in their love play he whispered something in her ear. At first she didn't hear. She stopped moving, looked into his face, and asked him to say it again. Again he whispered and again she didn't hear.

'Speak up, speak up, my darling,' she teased. 'We're each and every one a free man.'

'Tie me up,' he whispered.

'Tie you what?' She was startled.

'Tie me up, tie me up. Bind me. Hold me down. Control me. I want to be told what to do.'

Mildred at once decided not to take him seriously. 'Tie you up? Tie you up? I'll eat you up first.' And she began to bite him and pretend she'd not understood what he'd asked. So, exhausted they became, it's true, but when done, the sweetness, for Mildred at least, had soured. Even more so when, once again, he grooved his fingers into her body so viciously, so insistently, that she had to move from the bed to get out of reach when he refused to listen to her verbal pleas to stop.

She sat on a stool by the dressing-table and looked at him lying on his back staring up at the ceiling. What could she say to him? It was difficult because as yet she could not understand what was happening. Suddenly, in a tone of voice quite unsuited to the moment *as she felt it*, he said: 'That *was* an extravagant gesture wasn't it? A sports car! Humph!'

It was unbelievable. He seemed totally unaware of the effect he'd had upon her. He was thinking it was all a game.

'Sports cars! Wine stocking! Book collecting!' He looked up at his bewildered wife. 'You'll catch cold, come back to bed.'

She crept in beside him.

'Still', he continued, 'a man ought to be allowed to lapse into manias. It's no good a man like Jock Lamb telling me off. I'm too old to be told off.' He turned to his wife. 'I don't suppose he made you feel uneasy, you're tougher than I am, but he made me, with his – his unyielding principles, his – his – his moral-flexing. That's what it is: a flexing of all those iron muscles of morality. All to shame *my* moral flabbiness. Damn him! Not very enjoyable. Who wants friends like that?'

He turned over to sleep, backing his back to his wife. 'But we must invite him again,' he said, 'you know that, don't you? No quarrelling, we'll avoid that, but friends are precious, must invite him again.'

Which he did. And it was even more disastrous.

Jock came, smiling the flinching smile of a friend who remembered the fight and feared for its repetition. His wife at once began talking about the problems of the rising cost of living, as though there was no tension at all. They drank pale ale – Mildred stuck to her vodka – and spoke to one another as though they were strangers patiently waiting to discover something in common. Sheridan had discreetly removed some of their new acquisitions, though he felt that to be a kind of capitulation, and over the meal conversation drifted to the new education act which raised the school-leaving age to sixteen.

It was a strange conversation in that both knew there were aspects of education over which they disagreed and both tried avoiding them by sticking only to aspects they felt certain they were safe with. It was difficult. The comprehensive system for example. Sheridan believed in it in principle but had not sent his children to such a school.

'I can't sacrifice my children on the altar of *my* principles,' he argued. 'Those girls are bright, very bright, and they've got to be challenged. If the entire system were comprehensive, fine! But it's not. And I'm not going to place them where not only are the majority of a lower standard but the bloody teachers even despise children who are of a higher one!'

Jock had understood – he also felt insecure in that he'd no children of his own – but he believed a principle to be a principle. So they tried to avoid the areas they both knew might now lead to an explosive quarrel. It was no good. Sheridan, unleashed by drink, found himself again attacking the Left to which, as nothing else, he thought he had a profound spiritual attachment.

'We stick to our aspirations and attitudes more because they make us seem such "good people". But do they reflect an adult view of reality? Do they, hell! You think *I* want a world full of people buggered up because they can't be what they could be? That leads to violence. I'd be mad. Of course I don't. But not even the most ideal society is going to help a loser forget he's a loser. Believe me! The knowledge of failure is inherent in the act of failing. Yes! Inherent! And you insult the failed concert pianist by saying to him, "There! there! Never mind, you've got a sweet nature." Or forget the failed pianist. Take the boy in our office. We've got a boy in our office who I know wants to be like me – a first-class heating engineer. But will he be? Never! As sure as eggs is eggs I know he'll never be more than a competent draughtsman of small jobs. Never! Poor bastard!'

'How can you be so sure?' Jock shouted. 'About any human being how can you be so damn sure what they can or cannot do?'

Sheridan replied with absolute conviction fortified by the abandon accompanying drink: 'Just as *you're* sure that in any crowd of people, there are some you want to know and some you never ever, never ever, want to know. You make judgments. Assessments. You accept. You reject. A little computer inside you made up of experience and intelligence goes click, click, click!

and you know. Loser! Winner! A man's chemicals. They tell you. Now – go and make a just world for losers.'

There was a long silence after that outburst, the impact of which boomeranged and stunned Sheridan with infinitely more devastation than his old friend. He knew at once he'd articulated something which was to be another landmark in his tumbling, tumbling. He'd always believed in a society whose climate of social relationships would allow each man to be content with what he was. Though the bricklayer might know his skill was not as brilliant or satisfying as, say, the draughtsman, yet he, the bricklayer, might have other qualities: of making people laugh, or the persuasive power to turn a quarrelling couple into a tolerant one. So he'd thought. But now he wasn't sure. The bricklayer might well contribute to the levity of a gathering but somewhere he'd know the worth of bricklaying alongside draughtsmanship. After all, he'd surely not say to his son: 'Be a bricklayer, that's the life, my boy!' Intellectuals and artists may be quite happy if their rebellious sons wanted to be bricklayers – but that was in the safe knowledge they'd equipped their sons with opportunities to be something else when the phase for navvying passed. Like the ghost of a past truth he'd always feared would haunt him, he felt himself becoming too wise too late. The depressing conclusion faced him: if men could never be equals wasn't it unfair to create equal opportunities in which their inequalities would be seen?

It was an awful moment. A skin dropped from him. Not only did he see men as unequal, he felt relief that it was so, and the sense of relief disgusted him. His soul turned grey with fear. He'd not been a socialist for a long time.

That night, in bed, the room swimming a little, he became frightened of his children inheriting such conflicts, of the growing anarchy in the world, of the numbing of his capacity for outrage, of the thinning of his beliefs. As the weeks and the months passed he became lethargic, slothful, he dozed in chairs, left books half-read, and lost all curiosity about his family. Sometimes he still picked up Mildred's hand to caress it but his attention drifted. God knows where. Certainly out of her presence, for his grip became damp and limp. The only emotion able to animate him was that of hatred for his antiques which, in a frenzy, he sold at not much profit. The final humiliation: he'd been such a tiny speculator.

Once, after they'd made love, he cried, for no reason it seemed, just wept like a baby. And from then on did so again and again, the spasms in his groin releasing more, it seemed to her, than seed; releasing also a profound awareness of all that was now beyond his control. He didn't soar triumphant with his coming but caved in, shrivelled quickly, like a burnt-out sheet of celluloid. It became distasteful, contemptible. The jokes about fear had crystallized.

Then, one night, he snuggled up not to embrace her but as though – yes, she had to use the word – 'clawing' for comfort. And this time when she pushed him away he seemed to lose control and punched his head into the pit under her arm as if trying to enter her body, in the way young lambs greedily pump and push into their mother's teats for food.

'My God! I *am* frightened of everything,' he confessed to his wife, hoping honesty would win tender understanding. 'Now I really am.'

And once he said this his wife knew what it was had worried her in the early days of his metamorphosis: his affection had had more to do with what he seemed to need than with what he wanted to give her. It had not been love, it had been desperation. His honesty won no tenderness. She was not the sort of woman to respond maternally to a man's desperation, but cooled and turned away. And the tumbling, tumbling stopped.

*1972*

# POOLS
## A Short Story

Very slowly Mrs Hyams took her card, number eight, from its slot, handed it to the time-keeper and stepped out of the clothing factory into Brick Lane. As she walked home the evening smells of the East End met in her nostrils and mingled with the damp foggy air peculiar only to London at that time of the year.

Winter is a long time going, she thought, and so engrossed was she that it was some seconds before she realized she had turned into Flower and Dean Street instead of Fashion Street. She paused just past Katie's greengrocer shop and was, for the moment, lost. It was many months since she had come into this street despite its being the one next to her own. Just like a backyard, she thought.

She was about to retrace her steps when the idea occurred to her to pay a visit to Mrs Levy. It would be only for a few minutes for tonight was Wednesday night and she had many things to do at home. But she must see the old lady, especially as the Passover was so near.

Mrs Hyams continued, then, down Flower and Dean Street, nodding along the way at people she knew, and stopped by at one of the shops. There she bought a box of matzos, a quarter of a pound of soft cheese, some chopped liver, butter, a loaf of bread and a box of fancy biscuits. With these she crossed the road and walked to the last but one block of Nathaniel Buildings. It was dark now and, with caution, for the lamp was not very bright, she picked her way down the uneven steps to the cellar room where Mrs Levy lived. She knocked and called out, 'Mrs Levy?' There was no reply. The second time she knocked and called out she placed her ear near the door. 'Mrs Levy?' There was a sound of a bed creaking and soon some feet rubbed their way towards her.

'Who is there?' a little voice asked.

'Me, Mrs Levy, me—Mrs Hyams.' She heard the rattle of the latch and the door opened.

A very small woman with blue, watery eyes poked her head round the corner. Behind her the room was in darkness. She blinked for a few seconds and then, recognizing who it was, switched on the light and opened the door wider. Once in, with the door closed, Mrs Levy stepped back, drew her fingers to her mouth and in Yiddish said, as though speaking to somebody beside her, 'Ooh, look!' and grinned, showing her few decayed teeth. With childlike excitement she offered a seat to Mrs Hyams.

Mrs Hyams sat down and Mrs Levy placed herself on the edge of the bed, which was strewn with odds and ends of covering. The furniture was almost indiscernible in the dim light of the naked electric bulb. Behind Mrs Hyams, farther back into some dark corner, was an old deal table littered with an assortment of unopened tins of soup, jars, cardboard boxes and papers. A sideboard stood on three legs, littered with dirty pans; on the mantelpiece was a glass case containing a stuffed bird and, curiously, a pile of pipe cases. Nothing had changed.

Mrs Levy was about sixty now, four foot ten in height, plump, with large eyes that seemed to express amazement at what was going on around her, staring the way a baby does who cannot quite get over the shock of being born. Her lips were wet and sagged and her tongue slithered about her gums. She was still pale. They spoke in Yiddish.

'*Nu?*' Mrs Levy opened up her hands. 'How are you? Why haven't you been to see us? It's a year now, you haven't been. Such a long time.' She put her hand to her face and rocked it from side to side. 'Such a long time.'

'My daughter had a baby,' Mrs Hyams said.

'A baby?' Mrs Levy gave herself a pleased little hug; she always felt honoured that Mrs Hyams came to see her. 'A boy she had or a girl?'

'A boy, Mrs Levy, a boy.'

'And she's all right, the daughter; and the boy, he's all right?'

'The boy', Mrs Hyams said, leaning intimately forward and touching her hair, 'has blond hair.' Mrs Levy leaned forward with her. 'And his eyes, Mrs Levy, are blue,' and she leaned back as if to emphasize the fact, and Mrs Levy copied her movements and leaned back as well. They both smiled.

'It's so long since you have been,' said Mrs Levy again. Mrs Hyams lifted her shoulders and looked away; this meant—there has been no time. They were silent a few seconds. Then:

'Look,' said Mrs Hyams, bringing out the few things she had bought. 'I've brought you some food, it will be Passover soon.' One by one she placed the foodstuff on the table and opened them up that Mrs Levy might see.

'For me? For me you brought this? Ah, chopped liver. Now that *is* good. I thank you, thank you. Really good. *You* made it? You yourself? Is it dear? You should not. You cannot afford it. I'll give you some money. Is there any borsht? A good drop of borsht?'

'No borsht, Mrs Levy.'

'Ah, never mind, I'm not short, you know.' She grinned all the time, every now and then adjusting the shawl on her head or pushing away a lock of hair. She was almost purring. For some half an hour longer the two women continued talking.

Mrs Hyams told her friend that now she too lived alone, for

her daughter had gone to Bermuda where her husband had a post as a scientist in a factory; and her son lived outside London and could only come to see her once a week. Mrs Levy nodded her head in commiseration. She nodded most of the time for one reason or another, but mostly it was by way of indicating that this, this was the way the world is. 'And your husband ... ' she nodded slowly to acknowledge the terrible fact that he was killed in the war. 'And my husband ... ' said Mrs Hyams, and she nodded once or twice thereby finishing the sentence.

'So now at least come down to us more often,' Mrs Levy said. 'We're always in, you know.'

'Why don't you go out a little?' Mrs Hyams asked her. 'In the fresh air go. You are down here all the time.'

'Wouldn't we like to,' Mrs Levy replied, 'but now it's cold and we have nothing warm. We cannot go out like this.' She spread her arms wide to reveal the same old rags she had been wearing for many years. Mrs Hyams nodded.

Soon the atmosphere began to depress her; she could stay in the room no longer.

'I thank you, thank you,' Mrs Levy said at the door.

'Look after yourself,' said Mrs Hyams.

'We shall be well,' replied the old lady.

Mrs Hyams thought only of making her way home for it was cold. At the bottom of the stairs of No 43 Fashion Street she paused for breath. Downstairs in the basement the furrier was still working and so were the buttonmakers in the shop in front.

As she started to climb the steps a sound of feet jumping two stairs at a time came towards her. Before she knew what had happened, a young boy jumped to her side, snatched her bag from out of her hands and ran up to the top landing where she lived. 'You'll break your little neck one day,' she cried as she proceeded to follow him. 'Won't!' he cried back. He was on his

way down again, but this time he slid along the banister and
stopped on the landing below outside his own flat, where his
mother was waiting.

'I saw you coming,' said Mrs Hickory, 'so I waited till I heard
you start and then —'

'So that's no good,' Mrs Hyams smiled. 'I've got your chicken
in the bag.'

'Mervin,' said Mrs Hickory, and Mervin ran upstairs again
to bring back the bag. Mrs Hyams handed her friend the chicken.
'Such a lovely chicken,' she said.

'Cup of tea?' Mrs Hickory asked.

'No thank you, no. There is so much I must do.' She pinched
Mervin's nose and made her way up to the top landing. She was
puffing now. As she took out the key to her door Mrs Hickory
called up, 'Mrs Hyams, thank you!' She did not wait for a reply.
Some seconds later, just as Mrs Hyams was about to hang up her
coat, her neighbour called again. 'Mrs Hyams?' This time she
added nothing for Mervin appeared with something in his hand.
'Letter!' he said and ran off. That family, Mrs Hyams thought,
has not said a whole sentence between them since they've been
here.

She looked at the envelope; the foreign stamp on it told her
that it was from her daughter. She did not hasten to open it but
laid it behind one of the brass candlesticks on the mantelpiece
until she was ready to read it. The first thing she did was to light
the fire she had laid before leaving for work in the morning.
This done she changed into some slippers, went out to the landing to put some water on to boil and then set about making
herself some eggs and chips. While the chips were frying she
laid the table for herself, turned on the radio to hear the news
headlines and then put more coal on the fire.

It was while she was doing this that Mrs Hyams's thoughts
returned to Mrs Levy, for she suddenly recollected that Mrs

Levy had no fire. *That* was why the old lady had been in bed with all those clothes on.

Her memory was thrown into rusty gear and she recalled for the first time in many years how Mrs Levy had looked when she first saw her. Almost thirty-five years ago, when Mrs Hyams was a girl of twenty and her husband, who lived in Flower and Dean Street, was courting her, she had seen this beautiful young woman of twenty-five. What was outstanding was her carriage and the proud way she walked. The young woman, daughter of a poor family in Bessarabia, was brought over to England by her rich, elderly uncle who married her. She was so lovely then, Mrs Hyams thought, with some horror, but so green. Her husband, she recollected, used to make cigarettes; he had treated her as a princess; he did the shopping, the cooking, the housework. When she was thirty, he died. Then what happened? Mrs Hyams wondered. She could remember the beginning and knew the ending, but the years between, these she had lost. It was this sharp contrast that gave her such an odd feeling. For the memory of the young Mrs Levy was a memory of the young Mrs Hyams, and she suddenly felt very, very lonely.

It was some minutes before she could move from the fireplace to attend to the chips. At last she did move and muttered to herself—I will. I *will* put Mrs Levy on my list. Why she had not done so before she could not think and felt rather ashamed and guilty. This evening I will place her before my own holiday. And thus decided Mrs Hyams sat down to eat her eggs and chips.

She chewed her food without interest. Odd thoughts passed through her mind: such as Mrs Levy asking for borsht; Mervin sliding down the banister; her son would be along to supper in two evenings' time—as on all Friday nights; what had her daughter written. She was conscious of the silence. She could think with a lot of noise around her, read too, but the silence always disturbed her. Sometimes she moved simply that something should happen in the room.

Towards the end of her meal she began to hurry, eager now to read the letter from Bermuda; or was it that she could not bear to be doing the same thing for long? She collected the dirty dishes, having drunk the remainder of her tea standing up, and took them outside to the little table on the landing. She would wash up when the letter was read. Then she returned, cleared away the rest of the table that had been so carefully set out and sat in an armchair by the fire to read.

It was a letter like any other letter but the mother heard the words she read and saw each scene. Occasionally she would laugh to herself or give a low, long hum, showing how well she understood her daughter's feelings. When she came to the paragraph concerning her grandchildren she cooed and hugged herself and murmured – bless them, bless them. Soon the heat from the fire began to affect her and slowly, after a few sad, sudden starts, her head sank to her left shoulder and was still.

After some minutes Mrs Hyams awoke. Her first thought was to get up from the chair and attend to her very important task, but she got no further than laying her hands on the arms of the chair. Instead she sat back and lifted the letter once more to read. One thing she could not understand. What foolishness had taken her daughter away from her mother's care and advice? Mrs Hyams spoke aloud to herself. 'So what has she gained?' She turned to the fire and asked with her hands. 'So what, tell me!' Then she caught herself talking to herself and smiled. 'Such madness!' She rose, feeling oddly pleased with her own humour, and placed the letter behind the candlestick laughing and muttering, 'Oi yoi, Mrs Hyams you, what a you, Mrs Hyams!' But in bringing her hand down from replacing the letter she accidentally knocked a glass ashtray to the floor. She jumped, stared at the broken pieces for a few seconds as though not certain what had happened and then, after trying very hard to swallow down lumps in her throat, gave in and wept.

It was a long time since Mrs Hyams had cried. She hated tears; tears for her were weakness. Now she moved into the bedroom as though to hide from the presence of life which the fire in the front room suggested. There she sat on the edge of the bed with her eyes closed and choked with the effort not to cry. It was a battle soon won. It was because I saw Mrs Levy today, she told herself as she blew her nose. I really must do something for her. What kind of people are we to let a woman like that go down. Before returning to the other room she looked at herself in the mirror to make sure her face would not betray her. For some odd reason she poked her tongue out at herself and then, suddenly embarrassed at her own foolishness, she got up abruptly and sheepishly, as though people were around her.

With a brisk, renewed vigour the broken pieces of glass were collected, the dishes washed up and order restored to the room. This done, she stood on a chair by the window and closed the curtains; her movements were mechanical. From a small glass cabinet she took a pen and a bottle of ink; from behind one of the candlesticks withdrew an orange envelope; and from inside a white, bulbous china vase pulled out a folded sheet of lined foolscap. These things she laid in order on the table. Satisfied that she had forgotten nothing, she moved to the door and locked it. It was Wednesday night.

From the moment that Mrs Hyams locked the door, everything she did was done in complete earnestness. There was no doubt in her movements, nor did her mind for one moment question her actions. Mrs Hyams was about to fill in her weekly football coupon and she believed that, sooner or later, but undoubtedly, she would win £75,000.

She took her place in the same chair and first of all opened out the folded sheet of paper. It was headed:

*Things I must do with my £75,000*

1. Buy a house large enough for my daughter, my son, their families and me to live in so that we are all together.

2. Present them with the money they need to live their lives.

3. Give my brothers Hymie, Stanley and Martin £3,000 each.

4. Give my friend Lottie £1,000. And also Maurice, Jackie, Gertie.

5. Spend £20 on a holiday in a little seaside village.

6. Buy myself a pair of fur-lined boots for winter.

7. Pay back £10 to Steve Isaacs.

And so on. A long list of numbered items with each detail carefully written out, and changes seriously made as to the relative importance of certain articles of clothing.

Now she carefully scrutinized her list and made one more correction. In between items four and five, that is to say after giving £1,000 to Lottie, Maurice, Jackie and Gertie and before allotting £20 for her holiday, she wrote:

5. Put aside £5,000 to help Mrs Levy.

Then she folded up her list and laid it aside.

Filling out the coupon was reasonably easy, but Mrs Hyams spent a great deal of time on it, starting first with her copy coupon. She staked her money only on the Treble Chance column, and on this she gambled two shillings and sixpence each week. Meticulously she described her 'O's in the little squares and carefully she wrote out her name and address—not forgetting to place an 'X' in the right place, for she wished for no publicity when she won. The thing she was most careful about was not to make a blot or an erasure; her one horror was that they would disqualify her winnings no matter where that blot lay or despite that the erasure was obviously explicable. The pattern of her forecast was the same each week. She backed the same numbers regardless of which team played which and these very numbers were the ones her husband and son before her had used.

When her husband was alive nothing used to irritate Mrs Hyams more than Wednesday night, pools' night. Every week he would ask her to write it out for him because he was afraid of making a mistake; every week he asked her whether or not he should change the numbers he used. 'Will Stockport and Wolves draw, do you know?' he would ask. 'If I knew,' she replied, 'I'd tell you, fool!' When her husband died her boy took to doing the pools, but he married at nineteen and spent his first five married years abroad in the army. Soon afterwards her daughter married. In a short, perplexing period of time her whole family, the point of her existence, had broken up. It was some years before she regained her self-possession. Time and routine hardened her; life moved in her despite herself. She forced pleasures in trivialities, making do with the remains. Soon the sense of loyalty with which she took up the pools gave way to a sense of imperativeness. She *must* win the pools because with this money she would piece together the ruins of her family. This gave to her a calm such as a wonderful secret can give; a calm disturbed only by loneliness, when she would hurry to her brothers or a friend.

That night Mrs Hyams spent a longer time than usual filling out her coupon. She became another woman, even to look at. The intense concentration she used showed in her eyes and the way her skin curled above them; her tongue protruded and was held still by her lips, her glasses fell halfway down her nose.

But this evening the effort was too much. When she finished Mrs Hyams was very, very tired. Visiting Mrs Levy, receiving the letter, breaking an ashtray and then crying was a great deal to go through in an evening after work. Fortunately, tomorrow she was not working. At the age of sixty, three days a week was all she managed. Tomorrow she could lie in, which meant that the coupon had to be posted tonight in order to catch the first post Thursday morning. Liverpool was a long way and it had to be there in time. But there were all those stairs to walk down and climb up again. She could not face it that evening. Instead, she did something she had never done before. She called down to Mrs Hickory and asked if she minded sending her boy out to post a letter, please.

In the past anything that had to do with Mrs Hyams's football coupon she saw to herself, from filling to checking. Now she regretted breaking her rules the moment the boy had run off. Would he ever get there, she wondered. Might he not lose it or put it in the wrong box. He was only a boy after all. Mervin was away for a few minutes, which to her seemed hours; as soon as he returned she questioned him. Where had he taken it? Why was he so long? Had anybody stopped him? And not only on that evening but every other evening she catechized him until Sunday morning when she was able to check up and discover that it did not matter because that had not been her lucky week.

She did not check her coupon on Saturday nights. To her mind the results were too haphazardly arranged and one could not be certain if they were all correct. The order and certainty of a Sunday paper alone satisfied her.

This coming Friday she felt she had something interesting to say to her son about Mrs Levy. She spent all day in preparing the evening meal which that week consisted of a barley soup and a sweetly smelling *chuland*, to be followed by a trifle, and thought how best she could make her announcement so that her son would at once be interested.

Each week Mrs Hyams planned a sort of climax to her son's

weekly visit, for she felt, vaguely, that her boy, silly boy, was not always pleased to spend Friday night with her. Friday night was after all the night before *Shabbus*, a night when all good Jewish families were together, and she surely had a right to ask of him that she see her children for one day of the week. True, she had not brought him up religiously – still, Friday night was Friday night. So she looked for topics of conversation or made an issue of trivial occurrences, sometimes bought a present for him or his wife and always some chocolate for the grandchild.

At precisely six o'clock she could hear right from the bottom of the stairs a tiny voice calling, 'Grandma, boba, grandma, boba,' and it continued up until the time the little boy crept round the one but last flight and stood grinning at her. 'Lobus!' she cried and hurried down the remaining flight to pick him up in her arms. She kissed her son and her daughter-in-law and asked, '*Nu?* How are you?'

Stephen was a great deal taller than she, with a small head on his shoulders and a large nose as though to balance him. His disproportion would not have mattered had he been a gay person. As it was his heavy features were worsened by a bored, guttural look that so many young Jewish men have upon their faces. Stephen was bored with his job, his family and himself. He and his generation had not the stamina of their parents. He bent low and kissed her and replied with a slight impatience as though the question were asked too many times, '*Asoi!* Like so! What else?' and they all made their way into the little room which was laid out for supper.

As always happened, little Jeremy occupied most of the conversation, jabbering away about what he had done that week, what he had told God and what God had said to him; how he had seen a shooting star one night and if Jesus was a Jew, Grandma, why didn't he look like Daddy and have a black beard instead of a light one, and isn't this a lovely supper. Until he

talked himself to sleep and they laid him softly on the couch
while they themselves sat on till about ten in the evening.

Before sitting down Mrs Hyams took out a bowl of fruit and
nuts and sweets and asked if they had had enough to eat. 'A nice
supper,' said Stephen without looking up from the paper. 'You
always did like *chuland*,' said Mrs Hyams. Then they were silent
for some minutes. Miriam dozed in her chair, Stephen cracked
nuts with his teeth and continued to read the paper. Mrs Hyams
was wondering whether to mention her topic yet. She decided
not to and instead went out to the kitchen to put on some water
for tea. Then she was back in her chair looking at the fire.
Stephen cracked nuts and Miriam dozed on her other side. Mrs
Hyams was up again and from the mantelpiece handed her son
the letter from his sister.

'From Aida?' Stephen read the letter, shrugged his shoulders
and handed it back.

'A good letter, yes?' Mrs Hyams said. 'Have some sweets.'

'A good letter! A good letter!' he replied somewhat testily.
'It's a letter, so?'

'You think she's doing all right out there?'

'Why not?'

'She seems happy.'

'Look, she wants to live in Bermuda, so let her live in Bermuda.
I wouldn't, but it's her life. If she'd listened to me ... ' Stephen
wagged his finger and then cracked another nut.

'You're right, you're right,' his mother cooed. 'Why don't
you eat some fruit?' Again they were silent. Outside a low fog
hung in the narrow streets; a few doors away the moan of a
row was audible; the last cries of stubborn children echoed in the
air and a barrow from the market was wheeled over the uneven
stones, a weary, bored rattle.

They drank two cups of tea each and the conversation slugged
without much enthusiasm. About half an hour before the guests

were to leave Mrs Hyams made them their last cup of tea to be drunk with some apple strudle she had baked, and then said to Stephen,

'You know what, Stevee, I'm going to add something to my list.'

'Oh, Mum, not again. That silly list of yours. As if you were going to win £75,000.'

'I saw Mrs Levy on Wednesday.' Mrs Hyams ignored his outburst.

'So.'

'So nothing. So I'm just telling you. She makes me feel ashamed, Stevee. Such a place to live in.'

'Everyone she feels pity for, everyone. Have you seen a woman like her, have you? So now I suppose you're going to give Mrs Levy a couple of thousand pounds?' And here he smiled sweetly at his mother, feeling that he had to indulge her sometimes.

'£5,000,' she said, 'after giving £1,000 to Lottie, Maurice, Jackie and Gertie, and before I take £20 for my holiday.'

'Isn't that rather a lot?' said Miriam. 'She can't have so much longer to live.'

'No matter. £5,000.'

They gently picked Jeremy up in their arms and said their farewells. Mrs Hyams kissed the sleeping child and when they were halfway down the stairs she put out the light of the room that she might see them better from her window and wave. As she gazed she decided never again to mention her list or her pools to her children. Then she cleared up the last cups and went straight to bed, for the following day she had promised to look after Mrs Broom's two children while Mrs Broom attended the funeral of her sister-in-law. Mrs Broom was one of her neighbours two doors away in Fashion Street.

*

That following week was a depressing week. It rained almost every day. Returning from work on Wednesday night after the slow hours at the machine the little woman seemed reluctant to go home. At such times the East End impressed its slum upon her more than usual; the smells, which at moments were friendly, made her sick. The dirty sky fell over the buildings and seemed only an arm's length away. Brick Lane in particular was a gutter. People rushed past and cars splashed her. Not even the market called to her. And so, in this inhuman street, on this inhuman day, Mrs Hyams lost, with good nature, her good nature.

Feeling that she ought to see Mrs Levy once more, she stopped at the top of Flower and Dean Street. But she changed her mind. 'No, I won't go. Can I help it if Mrs Levy is unhappy? I'm unhappy. So what! So who cares? So Mrs Levy can wait, she can. I'm no angel!' And with this ill-temper she returned to her rooms.

It was pools night tonight, but she was in an odd mood. Having eaten her supper and spread her coupon before her, Mrs Hyams felt suddenly hopeless. 'Why', she asked herself, 'should Mrs Hyams win £75,000? What is so special about this Mrs Hyams and her family that is not so special about another Mrs Hyams and her family?' She laid down her pen. 'Finished! Not another penny.' Then she stood up and moved to the fireplace, which she poked irritably. Confronting herself in the mirror she waved the poker at her image. 'You, Mrs Hyams, you! You *mishiginah*, you! Every time you post your coupon five other people post it in just that second. And how many seconds are there?' She nodded to herself. 'And how many boxes are there?' Again she nodded. 'And everybody thinks that for their little penny they're going to get £75,000. You know that, Mrs Hyams?' She sank into the armchair still holding the poker. 'It's such a big world. Who's going to give you all that money? You break your heart every week. You want meat pies in the skies.' This time it was a very sagacious nod and she paused as though to digest fully what she told herself; then she whispered, moving her head so slowly that it almost nodded her to sleep, 'We got no real dreams any more.' She shrugged her shoulders at the fire. '*Nu?*' she asked herself in Yiddish. 'So what shall I do else?'

She turned back to the table and was about to sit down when a sudden answer came. 'Tear it up I can do, that's what!' She lifted the coupon as if to throw it on the fire. But the moment of rebellion died too soon. Again she said in Yiddish, 'Indeed, what shall I do else!' Methodically, with great concern, her tongue protruding a little between her lips, Mrs Hyams completed her pools coupon, not forgetting to put an 'X' in the place to indicate she wanted no publicity when she won.

But the winter does pass; even in the East End the sun on any building imprints its spring; and Itchy Park, that small cemetery between the high church in Commercial Street and Christ Church School in Brick Lane, where the tramp sits and the child plays, has trees that leaf and a green smell.

And with spring came a little surprise to Mrs Hyams. For helping them through the hardships of last winter and many winters before, the neighbours in Fashion Street rewarded the obliging old lady by collecting among themselves some £20. This they presented to her and hoped it would be enough to pay for a holiday that summer. Mrs Hyams was embarrassed at first and refused: 'I've done nothing. I've never heard of such a thing. I don't need the money!' But eventually she succumbed. 'For me? £20? Such a lot of money.'

When they left her Mrs Hyams returned to her room and laid the £20 in neat piles of five on the table before her. 'Such a lot of money,' she repeated. She sat for a long time feeling a great love for humanity and herself, then she rose, went to the mantelpiece and withdrew from behind the candlestick her precious list. Between the item giving £5,000 to help Mrs Levy and that allotting herself a pair of fur-lined boots for winter was the reminder that she should spend £20 for a holiday in a little seaside village. This she now crossed out. 'Why not?' she said to herself.

For many days she gossiped excitedly to her good neighbours about her holiday.

'Going on your own?' they asked.

'Why not?' she replied proudly. 'I'm old enough!' They asked her where she planned to go. 'I'm not sure,' she answered. 'Not yet, I'm not sure. But I'll tell you where I'm not going,' she added in a whisper as though it were blasphemy. 'I'm not going to Southend and I'm not going to Bournemouth and I'm not going to Brighton!'

The only person who offered any advice where in fact she could go was the young, bespectacled, arty-looking man in the post office where she bought her postal order. He knew just the place to suit her.

'A little guest-house near to the seaside village of Burnham Deepdale on the north coast of East Anglia, and you can get there straight from Liverpool Street Station. Beautiful, Mrs Hyams; some friends of mine, you see. Far from the madding crowd —'

'The which crowd?'

' —peace, rest, the smell of the salt air. Come and go as you please. Sands nearby, cliffs and the North Sea stretching like eternity before you.'

'Like who?'

'Only five guineas a week and excellent food.'

'Kosher?'

'Hardly,' the young man smiled.

'Still, perhaps it doesn't matter,' Mrs Hyams said. 'Now is modern times, we must do like the Romans do, eh? It sounds very nice,' she added. It sounded so nice, in fact, that Mrs Hyams eventually decided that there was where she would spend her vacation, in late September, so as to miss the main holiday rush.

The young man in the post office, with the utmost good nature, undertook to write to his friends and make all the necessary arrangements, while Mrs Hyams, adopting a carefree attitude, insisted on nothing in the terms except the appearance of a Sunday newspaper. It can all take care of itself, she decided, and when she handed the young man ten guineas to pay for a two-week sojourn, she said, '*Na!*' and placed complete trust in him.

The seaside village of Burnham Deepdale turned out to be just as Mrs Hyams wanted it to be. Each house was a different shape, the streets were narrow and most were cobbled. Here and there was a thatched roof and despite the appearance of about three boarding houses in what was presumably the main street yet there was no sign of commercialization.

For some minutes Mrs Hyams stood outside the station and wondered what was missing. She felt something should happen. There she stood, a case at her side, in the white air with her head cocked to one side. Soon the hiss of the sea slowly and rhythmically rolled into her ears. She had left behind the noise of London, that was it. She felt very happy.

The hosts at the guest-house, which was two miles away from the village, proved, however, to be a little queer. Mr and Mrs Mortimer were a young couple. They had three children who managed to be in so many different places at once that they seemed to multiply themselves each minute. Mr Mortimer was partly bald, wore a white T-shirt, a red scarf, blue jeans and sandals and smoked a pipe. Mrs Mortimer wore a blue T-shirt,

a white scarf, red jeans and sandals and smoked a cigarette. The
two youngest children, boys aged three and four, were naked;
the third, a girl aged six, wore only knickers. Mrs Hyams was
not what they had expected, and the young couple were not
what Mrs Hyams expected. After saying, 'How do you do, I'm
Mrs Hyams,' she pointed to the children, who were staring
at her, and raising her hand to her mouth asked with
concern, 'They won't catch cold?' This brought a bellow of
laughter from Mr Mortimer, in which everyone soon joined
and the first awkward moment was passed and forgotten. Mrs
Mortimer cuddled her guest and gaily showed her to her room,
while the guest, determined to remain carefree, took in the
Bohemian atmosphere which was as new as the fresh air and so
part of it.

It was Friday. Mrs Mortimer told her that there had been no
other guests for the past week, but more were expected on the
following Monday. Mrs Hyams had a whole weekend in which
to find her way around. She would be an old inhabitant by the
time the others came, and that position just suited her.

'Now this really is summer,' said Mrs Hyams on being led into
her room. It was a corner room that had windows on two walls
of the house. The sun spent all but the evening in it, and just
now was bandying its full light from wall to wall. Here she felt
at home and that the city amounted to not very much after all.

Perhaps more than anything this occupied Mrs Hyams's
excited mind: that four hours ago, maybe more, she was in
London and now she was in a strange bedroom looking at the
sea a mile away. She said the name 'Fashion Street' to herself,
then murmured, 'Burnham Deepdale.' She smiled. She thought
and spoke the name 'Mrs Rosenberg' then 'Mrs Mortimer'. The
different images that these two names conjured up amused her
and she continued, muttering to herself, 'Bigales — shrimps.
Shmultz herring — Mr Mortimer. Gefülte fish — bacon. Tochas —

Mrs Mortimer. Petticoat Lane—Burnham Deepdale.' And all the time she giggled to herself and worked herself into the most delighted of humours. Why, she could hardly remember what Mrs Levy looked like. Rising, she looked into the mirror and grinned sheepishly. 'Ah you, Mrs Hyams, you!' she said, then turned to look at her room. It was a nice room. Nothing had gone wrong.

Mrs Hyams washed herself and, despite that she was tired, surprised Mr Mortimer by asking if there was a café nearby where she could have some tea and cake. There was none, but a bus was due within ten minutes which would take her to the village.

'Such a long time you wait for the bus?'

'Run every hour,' Mr Mortimer replied.

'Oh, my Gawd!' exclaimed the astonished Londoner. 'And you don't complain to the company or something?'

Mr Mortimer, not knowing whether to take the last suggestion seriously or not, managed to smile and pointed out where the bus would stop.

The Mortimers considered their guest quite strange, but, 'Nice, darling, and amusing rather.' It was, they supposed, understandable to want to wander out as soon as you came to a guest-house on holiday. A little odd, however, not to change or even unpack. They spent some time discussing her. She had not even left word as to whether she would be in for supper or not, though no doubt she would—it was part of the fee—and accordingly Mrs Mortimer prepared the food.

It was a cold supper, but even had it been hot it would have become cold, for Mrs Hyams had not returned at the hour when it was time to eat. She had left at four o'clock and by nine o'clock the Mortimers had become concerned. They decided to wait until ten thirty when the last bus came from the village, and then if she was not on that they would contact the police.

There was no need to have worried, however, Mrs Hyams was on the last bus. She was very much alive and greeted her running hosts as though she had known them for a long time. But she was extremely tired and told them, 'Wait till we get in the house; such a time! I'll tell you.'

Once settled, Mrs Hyams closed her eyes. 'It's so-oo lovely.' Without opening them, she continued, 'Such sand and stones. The air — you feel you want to rub your face on it.' Her eyes opened. 'I walked twenty miles from the village to the lighthouse along the sands —'

'Two miles,' corrected Mr Mortimer.

' — and I looked in all the shops. Oh, pretty shops! And I lay underneath the sun and — guess what! I bought a sixpenny cornet and I sucked it all!' The couple laughed. Mrs Hyams lay back again and closed her eyes once more. 'Then I went and had a meal and then I went to pictures.'

'To pictures!' they exclaimed.

'Sure, why not? Nothing else to do.'

Mrs Hyams drank the cup of tea that was made for her and with a tired, aged ecstasy reiterated her pleasure at being there, and retired to her room. She would leave unpacking till the morning; all she did was open her bag, make sure the copy of her pools coupon was there and with it the entry form for the following week, undressed and delved slowly into a deep, comfortable sleep.

The following morning the long arm of a tender sun touched open her eyes. A sensation that was too sweet to contain made her hide her head under the blankets. When eventually she emerged she could see through the window on her right side half the sun and a clear, blue sky. She had never seen it so blue before. She did not move, but stared till her eyes could hold the colour no longer, then she slid once more beneath the blankets and sighed so deeply that she coughed.

For the rest of the day the sky remained blue. Being the first
impression her mind received in the morning it affected all she
saw. Even the mad lanes and the crazy cottages were a sweet,
ethereal, dreamy blue.

She lay on the sands under a newspaper, eating sandwiches
prepared for her by Mrs Mortimer, leaning against the hard
walls which looked like a village street placed on its side. A stray
dog came up to her as she ate and settled at her side as though
she had mastered it for years. But what enhanced the friendly
atmosphere of the little village even more was when a small,
muddy-faced boy, who had been standing watching her for
some minutes with his shy hands behind his back, suddenly
approached, as though having finally decided she was capable,
threw a ball to her, which she missed, and waited for her to
throw it back. Of course she bought him an ice-cream, and in
return he took her along the sands in the other direction from
where she had gone the day before and showed her a real cave,
one that harboured nothing more than some washed-up pieces
of green wood. To her great consternation the child then began
clambering over the rocks and returned with a nest of eggs.
'You'll take them back?' she asked him. 'Now, how would you
like it if I took you away from your mother, eh? But what
lovely eggs!' The child laughed, tiny laughter in all that sea.

Mrs Hyams returned for supper in the evening and spent two
slow hours writing to her son and her friend Mrs Cohen. To Mrs
Cohen she wrote simply:

My dear Mrs Cohen,
    It's much more than I expected here. Everything seems
like blue, and I am very grateful to you and Mrs Rosenbaum
and Mrs Jeremiah and all of you for the happiness you have
caused me. I wish you was with me in the sea. Such sea is
here is like somebody moved it there and could call for it

tomorrow. I can't tell you how it's so nice, but maybe being well in two weeks I shall tell you.

Your very good friend,

MRS HYAMS

To her son she wrote a long letter telling him not to worry, she would soon be back and, by the way, she fancied some pickled cucumber.

Mrs Hyams was awakened on Sunday morning by Mrs Mortimer, who entered carrying a tray of breakfast.

'Ah, hello and good morning, Mrs Hyams. *This* is not usual,' she smiled and laid the tray by the bed. 'But,' she added, helping Mrs Hyams to sit up, 'as you are our only guest at the moment, and as we think a special lot of you, we are making an exception.'

'You shouldn't,' said Mrs Hyams. 'I haven't had breakfast inside my bed for nearly ten years now.' She looked at the tray and noticed there was no Sunday paper as she had ordered. 'I suppose', she asked, 'the papers I ordered are downstairs?'

'Papers, Mrs Hyams?' exclaimed Mrs Mortimer. 'We don't read them in this house. Only the *Statesman* at weekends.'

'Has that got the football results?' Mrs Hyams asked. The young woman laughed. 'But I asked the post office man specially to order them.'

'Oh, Clinton? *He* said nothing. Papers are such a waste of money today. Lies, gossip, sports, etc. We just don't bother.'

'But I must have a paper,' Mrs Hyams said, as though it were surely obvious to everyone why she must have one.

'Perhaps you can get one in the village later on,' replied Mrs Mortimer. 'Now drink up, dear, and eat well.' And with that she went from the room, leaving Mrs Hyams dazed by this most unexpected blow. It was so silly not to have a newspaper in a house. How could she check her pools? The city had never let her down.

As though working out what had happened she sat, unmoving, propped up in bed. The sky was clear. A gull flew very close to the window. Somewhere one of the Mortimer children was crying, 'Mummy, Mummy.'

How could she check her pools without a Sunday paper?

The sun felt very warm on her arm. A slight breeze blew the curtain towards her. It was very quiet now. Only the sea brushed its hair with long, feminine arms, humming ecstatically to itself.

Confused between Fashion Street and Burnham Deepdale, wondering now how she came here, Mrs Hyams lost her way and could only close her eyes. She saw her coupon spread before her on the table at home, a Sunday paper at its side. 'I must have a paper,' she muttered, and so saying moved clumsily and hurriedly out of bed and dressed. She left the house, taking only her purse with her.

'I'm going to the village for a paper,' she told the surprised Mortimers on her way out. Mr Mortimer looked at his wife.

'White's may have some still, or Hoy's, eh, darling? But,' turning to Mrs Hyams and smiling, 'it's a small place. Can't chance many extras, can they? Still —'

'Oh, Mrs Hyams,' Mrs Mortimer spoke. 'Jonathan and I are taking advantage of the fact that we only have one guest. I know you won't mind. We're taking the children out for a picnic. Back about fourish, won't we, dear?' She turned to her husband, who nodded. 'But there is plenty to eat, cold salads and the like. You can find your way around, can't you?'

Mrs Hyams thanked them and walked very quickly to the bus stop, rolling slightly, like a sailor, though a bus was not due for many minutes. It was ten o'clock and the day was in its lovely innocence. But not the day's innocence nor the sky nor the scented air did Mrs Hyams notice. She must only hurry and try to find a newspaper. For how, she asked herself again, can I see if I have won my pools? And if I've won, how can I tell them when I don't know? If I don't tell them, she reasoned, I shall not get my money.

The bus drew up all too slowly and with a teasing gurgle continued, in holiday mood, to dribble happily along the road to the village.

The two shops, White's and Hoy's, had no papers left. 'You don't keep any back?' she asked. 'So if visitors come they can't have? They must go without?' She left the shops in disgust.

The streets were deserted. Sunday hung empty and pure over the village. Not knowing what else to do she walked towards the beach. Her steps took her to one of the boarding houses. She stopped outside and looked through the windows like a hungry, envious pauper, at the residents sitting in the lounge inside. They were all of them reading newspapers. Her first impulse was to walk in and ask to look at one. Shyness overcame her. How could she ask to look at a newspaper simply to check her pools? She felt ashamed and sheepishly moved away.

As she approached the other boarding house a young man came out reading a paper. At the gate he paused to digest more intently something that interested him. Mrs Hyams moved quickly.

'Excuse me, forgive me,' she said. The young man lowered his paper and smiled at her.

'Yes?' he asked.

She hesitated. 'Can you tell me the way to the beach?' she said instead.

In the indolence of the country she had been too free, intoxicated with the freshness of her change. At home she could rely on life, here nothing mattered.

Just as she was regretting ever having come on holiday she saw a boy on a bicycle delivering newspapers. It all happened very quickly. He had a spare paper and gave it to her. She gave him a shilling and told him to keep the change. As a child who laughs through its tears on being given the toy it had been forbidden to play with, Mrs Hyams hugged the newspaper and hurried, laughing, noticing the blue sky, smelling the air again, to a café that seemed to have opened only out of habit. She could now check her pools.

But her coupon was not with her. She had left it in her hand-bag in the bedroom. Or was it out of her bag on the floor? And had Mrs Mortimer swept it up? She must return at once. Slowly obsession followed upon urgency like the next man in the queue.

She waited twenty minutes for a bus to crawl up to her like a guilty dog. The conductor was the same who had brought her into the village. She fumbled with her money and gave him a farthing instead of a sixpence. The twopence change dropped to the floor. She laid the paper on the seat and bent to pick them up, but the conductor reached there before her and handed them back, saying what fine weather it was.

Was the coupon on the table or in her bag? She was so taken up with this thought that she noticed too late the bus go past the guest-house. Awkwardly she jumped up and asked for the bus to be stopped. Her thoughts and her actions betrayed her at each point, for in hurrying from the bus she forgot the paper and realized this only when she discovered that in fact her coupon was quite safe in her handbag.

Exhausted and frustrated, Mrs Hyams sank on to the bed and moaned like an old woman lamenting a death. Defeated at every turn, her holiday collapsed about her. She lost confidence. There remained only one thing to do – return to London.

To Mrs Hyams this seemed not only obvious, but simple, for surely Fashion Street was not far away, and there in London she could get a newspaper and check her pools. Hastily she

packed her bags, scribbled a note to the kind Mortimers and
waited for a bus to take her to the station. The conductor was
the same as had accompanied her on her previous two journeys.

So complete is the satisfaction of a final decision that one does
not consider alternatives; that is why Mrs Hyams did not think
to ask the conductor if he had picked up her paper which was
lying in his case at that moment; nor did she feel annoyed that
people in the carriage of her train were the proud possessors of
five different Sunday journals. Liverpool Street Station would
be filled with newsvendors. It was not that she was calm now,
but that a subdued hysterical smugness came over her. It was
the child again, happy with her promise of the toy, yet waiting
to burst into tears should anyone frustrate her more.

Mrs Hyams began thinking of her list and how lovely it will
be to fulfil all the items. £75,000 was a lot of money. But why
had she not been able to find a newspaper? It was such a common
thing. Perhaps it was a good sign. Of course. This is the way all
luck stories turn out. For ten years she had received her papers
regularly, but apart from an odd pound or so nothing big had
ever come of her weekly gamble. And now, now she had not
been able to find one she had won. She would reach London,
buy her paper and then send the telegram. Then she would go to
her son's house and discuss it all with him. She could not go
back to Fashion Street, the neighbours might be offended at her
quick return. That was life for you.

The train arrived later than she had anticipated. It was beginning to get dark. The smell of the station fitted sweetly into
place, but Mrs Hyams did not stop to savour her homecoming.
Had she done so she might have collected her wits and made
order out of the confused movement of traffic. As it was the
station loomed large and busy. People rushed and the noise grew
and subsided, rocking and heaving like a large woman breathing
in a nightmare. In and out of the crowds, having left her case

at the luggage office, she made her way to where the papers were usually sold. But the first stall was emptied and the second was deserted, and the third sold lascivious magazines, and the fourth had only soiled copies of last night's papers, a fifth had flowers and a sixth was packing up having just sold a last copy.

Where were the papers? Had London gone mad not to have news? I must send a telegram, she thought.

She wandered back into the station, too dazed to remember the little sweet shop at the corner of Artillery Row. It was so late and Liverpool was such a long way away. She muttered to herself, 'I must let them know I've won.'

Under the stairs near the entrance stood a row of telephone kiosks with their doors open like sentries at ease. Trembling now, she dialled 'O' and waited for a long time till the operator answered.

'Number, please?'

'This is Mrs Hyams of 43, Fashion Street, London, E1. Send a telegram and tell them I've won before it's too late.'

'You want telegrams, madam,' a soft voice at the other end said. 'Hold the line, please, I'll put you through.'

'Send a telegram to pools, please,' she cried to the new voice, and told them again her name and address.

'Which pool are you claiming, caller?' asked the operator.

'Penny Points—no, Treble Chance,' for a moment she was not certain. 'I've won £75,000, haven't I?' she asked, hoping that the man at the other end had in some way a connection with such a vast organization.

'Please place 3s. 9d. in the box, caller, and then press button A,' was all he replied.

This done, she tumbled out of the hot kiosk and stood for a second trying to control her excitement. It was all so much for an old woman. She was wondering what to do next when she noticed, fluttering on the floor, dirty and forgotten, the front

and back page of a Sunday newspaper. She was disturbed. The
reality at last of a newspaper emerged from another world and
vaguely threatened her. As if not content merely to remind her of
reality the paper fluttered again, demanding to be picked up.
Looking shyly around to make sure she was not being watched,
she bent down suddenly and retrieved it. It was today's. But
where could she go now to check her pools?

Nearby was the women's toilet. She entered. But she could
not check up there before the attendant and a long line of
hostile mirrors. There remained only one place. Once inside the
small cubicle, though alone and unseen, Mrs Hyams felt embarrassed as she pulled down the seat cover upon which to rest her
copy. Carefully she folded the newspaper leaving in sight in
the smallest space possible all the results she wanted. Then,
withdrawing a yellow pencil from her handbag she checked,
one by one, her entries on her coupon.

Now that the excitement was over she could not recollect
why it had ever been. Her feelings were bruised, but she and the
world were quite normal now. 'Why', she said to herself,
'should Mrs Hyams win £75,000 anyway?' She walked out of
the toilet into the huge dome of the station. 'Who is Mrs
Hyams?' she asked, walking towards the luggage office. Idly she
bumped into someone and said, 'I beg your pardon,' then
continued among the crowds and answered herself, 'She's no
one. She's nothing. So? *Nu?*'

*1955*

LOVE LETTERS ON BLUE PAPER

Victor wrote: 'Please come and see me. I've something of great importance to discuss with you. As soon as you can. Don't tell anyone.'

As Sonia opened the door to my ringing I looked to see if she knew why I'd been summoned. The once tall and ample York-shire girl with dark dramatic features whom some had thought mad, her gaiety having been so wild and unpredictable, was now a large, heavy old woman, withdrawn. Even so her hostile surprise surprised me. Why didn't she know I'd been called? She asked me to wait and went to the kitchen for a sponge. I wondered what *that* would be used for, and was reminded of the energetic twenty-four year-old, good-naturedly bullying the restless Marsden household into order and crying, 'Don't go anywhere wi' your hands empty! Little buggers! You hear me?' Her habits had remained, the spirit merely rumbled. She took me not into his study but upstairs to their bedroom.

He'd been ill.

'Maurice, lad!' He feigned astonishment. 'You! Why didn't you tell me you were coming?'

Sonia screwed her lips in scepticism as she moved ritualistically to wipe some egg that had caked on his drooping grey and nico-tined moustache. Ah! That's what the sponge had been for.

What had made Victor write instead of phone? Why hadn't he mentioned he was not well? Why pretend in front of Sonia he'd not written at all? Thirty years of marriage alerted her reflexes to his wishes and she left the room knowing he wanted to be alone with me.

'Take that chair. Throw those books on the floor. You've chosen a good day to come. Been rotten lately, not well at all. But today? Ha! Look at that sun! It's gotten right into me.' He ignored tensions, the existence of deceit and mystery, and pointed at the April sunlight which poured into the room. 'Wild, eh? Full of youth. Lovely!' He wrapped warm Yorkshire tones round the word 'louverly', closed his eyes and breathed deeply, which made him cough. 'Shouldn't be misled by sunlight,' he said between gasps, 'makes you want to take breaths you haven't got.' And he laughed.

But his greeting, not covering more than two or three minutes, had gone through a spectrum of emotions: anxiety at my arrival – could he carry through the pretence; the pretence itself, of mock surprise and unspontaneous pleasure; the guilt for deceiving the woman to whom he was married; joy for the sunlight; the distress of coughing. He was exhausted within seconds and lay back against a bevy of bright, white, semi-starched cushions, his chalky hair bushed out like needle rays of energy from a pale face, his black, coal-miner's eyes now seeming to go mad from their own intelligence.

He recovered quickly, beamed one of his mischievous smiles, as though the coughing had been a bit of music-hall fun, and croaked: 'You've come just at the right time, listen to this.' From a notebook he read:

The genuine creative instinct is and always has been a cele-bratory one. The earliest known forms of painting and ritual may have had to do with magic born of ignorance but beginnings should not be mistaken for truths. That a human activity was *begun* for one reason does not endow that reason with truth. There is nothing in the nature of beginnings which gives them the quality of inevitable correctness. We all know that such a thing as a *false* beginning exists ...

He corrected that last sentence while reading it and read it out again:

We all know of the existence of false beginnings. Art may have begun in the belief that the act of mimesis contained magical properties but once man discovered himself capable of the act he looked at himself in wonderment, delighted in it and thenceforth excelled in it only when his motivation was celebratory. This modest history of art will attempt to prove such.

I was on the point of asking was this his reason for calling me to see him, to announce he'd started the book he'd always talked about writing. But he wanted to pretend he hadn't summoned me. Let him. I would soon know why. He looked up, feverish with his own excitements, waiting for a response.

'It's a very good beginning.' I was impressed. 'And a very generous theory to want to prove. Congratulations for starting it. But first tell me why you're in bed.'

My question was ignored. A weary head sank back into its ample pillows, relieved but even more exhausted.

'It's rotten!' he said, 'Clumsy and illiterate. Like me. Written in the language of the negotiating table.' His manner had changed, mercurially, to anger. He turned, caught my look of anxious bewilderment and moved his mood yet again. 'But it *is* a beginning I suppose.'

This time, though, I saw the effort through the seductive smile.

Victor's passion was the visual arts, a sad passion hanging like a delayed and lonely blossom on an old bush whose other flowers had long gone. Canvases and sculptured heads – many of trade-union leaders which he hoped would one day be bought by their unions – leaned against walls or squatted on shaky surfaces waiting for homes, orphans of his brave battles to promote art to sceptical, tolerant but unimpressed labour colleagues. The ship-wrecked works cluttered his home now.

'Trouble is', he said, 'no one's interested in art. Even artists have been made to feel guilty: diminishing their roles like old-fashioned sinners, full of self-castigation. Everyone seems more obsessed by the way silly people have treated art than by the way great men have created it. And if you've not got even the artists on your side, well ... ' He seemed uncomfortable among his pillows and with irritation begun to pummel them into a new shape. The soft things were a scapegoat though. I moved to arrange them for him. This friendly act of assistance turned out to be a final straw. As I leaned over him he relinquished hold upon will-power and said: 'I'm dying, lad.'

He slouched his eyes at me like a tired, hunted stag indifferent to slaughter, stared at me staring, sympathetically nodded his head to see me so transfixed and said: 'Six months, nine months, a year. They're not certain. But soon.' He nodded again seeming to say, 'yes, you're shocked but imagine how I feel,' then turned away as though every living thing and especially I were to blame.

I believed him at once, froze at the shock and with unforgivable rudeness continued staring. Before me was a friend who knew the time of his own ending and there was nothing I could say. Not, 'don't be silly', not, 'are they sure?' not, 'maybe they've made a mistake.' I knew, certainly, that what he'd communicated was unalterable. There had been *no* mistake. They were sure, therefore he was sure and made me know it.

My silence was endless and unforgivable and my first words were to apologize for it.

'No,' he said, 't'were me, the way I told thee. Thoughtless.

What did I expect thee to do?' Bitterness and disgust lost their
edge in the soft, biblical tones of his Yorkshire dialect. I began to
babble: didn't believe it, mistakes had been made before, I could
tell him stories, *such* stories, doctors had calculated a year and
men had lived on and on and on.

'Maurice, don't bumble. I'm dying. It's myloid leukaemia. I've
waited three years for these last months. They've come. That's
that! Now, just let me talk.' He'd been preparing hard for this
hard meeting and was going to embark on what he'd rehearsed.

'Oh I'm frightened. No doubt about that. And bitter. Look at
it – that sun, those sounds, these books. Who'd want to leave all
that?' He picked up a newspaper. 'Despite all this!' His determined arms struggled noisily with the large sheets. '"Allegations
of torture to prisoners of war in North Vietnam. I.R.A. provos
pocket £150,000 of donations intended for arms." And did you
see this full-page advertisement appealing for help for students
being tortured in South Vietnam? Never stops, does it! "Man
batters child to death. Youths batter old man to death. Quarter
of London's homes without baths and heating. Soldier aged
nineteen shot in back in Belfast. Strikes throughout Spain.
Famine in India. Pit disaster."' He said it all in one breath which
made him cough and his irritation increase. But he squeezed his
contempt through the coughing: 'Still! Still, still, still! After
what we did. All we did.'

The coughing spun blue veins around his nose and produced
purplish hues about his face. He gave himself pause. 'And yet,' he
sighed, 'I don't care. I don't. I don't want to leave any of it. I'd
live with it all. Frustration, disillusion, sadness – the lot! Just so
long as I lived.' Still in a state of shock myself there was nothing
to do or say but let him continue. In his own time. Or not continue. Or ask me to go and come back another day.

'All those plans to travel. Ha! Retired me from the union just
in time didn't they, eh?'

He played with the sheet's edge, pulling its creases from under the blankets, pointlessly folding it and smoothing it down in front of him as though he was about to be inspected.

'I'll tell you a story.' He heaved into narration, his breath shuddering like the child who'd wept long and was now explaining why. 'Told me by the head of one of the largest unions in West Germany. Fantastic fellow he was, still is I suppose. God knows! Lose touch with them. You share a special conference or something together, you're bosom pals, take to each other better'n any of them at those dreary affairs – and we used to get some boring old sods at those affairs you know, self-righteous little functionaries they were, so when you met someone who had a bit of a twinkle in his eye, were vivid, you know, you'd latch on to him, stay together, crack jokes about the others, take it in perspective and then end up with all the bloody responsibility – where was I? Ah, Wolfgang! Wolfgang Heuder, dragged into the Wermacht when he was fifteen, last months of the war. I was probably chasing him in one of my tanks! It was him told me this story.

'Seems their regiment picked up a deserter, some poor scrawny old man who'd been out of the war because of flat feet or asthma or something but now they were taking in anyone who could hold a rifle. He'd had no appetite for the glorious Third Reich right from the start so he'd precious little urgency to die for it in its last gasps. Who would? And off he scarpered. He could smell defeat. But – he'd no energy. Food supplies low, foot-sore, wheezing – he was caught, court-marshalled, and sentenced to a firing squad. That depressed everyone it seemed. No one had stomach for it, not even the regiment commander. But he was an old soak, duty was duty, regulations regulations. There had to be a trial, it had to be a fair trial, there had to be a sentence, it had to be carried out. Victims of law and order when all law and bloody order were crumbling round them. Madness, eh?

'Still, the commander was an honourable man and he asked the prisoner if he had any last wishes. You know what the poor bugger asked for? A plate of barley soup! Wanted to eat before dying. To go off on a full stomach as it were. It were staple fare and there were some left to be heated up in the kitchens so they give it him. What he'd asked for. A plate of barley soup! And when it were finished, now listen to this, when it were finished he asked for another plate! That were unprecedented but – nothing in the rules to say a sentenced man couldn't have as much of his last request as he wanted, and rules were rules! Ha! So, another plate was called for and the man ate it slowly. And when he'd finished, yes, he asked for another plate and this time they had to wait while it was being made because they'd run out of the previous night's left-overs. And he ate. And he ate and he ate and he ate! Barley soup! More'n he wanted, more'n he could take. Anything, so long as it delayed the moment of his death. And you know what happened? The Russians came. The sentence couldn't be carried out. Everyone fled. He lived! He couldn't have known he'd live but some instinct kept him eating, eating to stay alive! I like that story. Wolfgang swore it were true. His regiment! He did the cooking, he says. Ha! Eating to stay alive! Simple!'

The story had agitated and distressed him. But then he looked closely at me and it was his turn to be anxious. Perhaps the tightness of my jaw muscles caught his attention; I was clenching my teeth in order to prevent myself from – what? Crying?

'I've given you a *real* shock haven't I lad? A real burden. You're all pale. That's terrible. What *was* I thinking of, daft old bugger.' It was absurd.

'Don't start being sorry for me!' I cried, 'for Christ's sake! That's madness!' I began to babble again: 'Victor! Oh, Jesus! Victor,' and took his hand. 'I wish at this moment I was a religious man, that *you* were a religious man. I wish I could tell you about an after-life, about heaven, about reincarnation, something!

What am I saying? It's monstrous! I'm sorry ... I ... ' He excitedly interrupted me.

'That's it! That's just it! *That's* why I wrote. Or at least that's *one* of the reasons, oooooh ... ' The moan died out like an air-raid siren whirring to a halt, relieved its shrill warning was confessed and over but totally disinterested in the follow-up. After a long pause, and as though he'd regretted calling anyone to discuss his 'reasons', he said: 'Why not go down and see if Sonia'll make us a cup of tea?' I stood up. 'She doesn't know,' he added. Then my legs became so weak that I stumbled, grabbed at the wall for support and had to sit again. This amused him. He laughed loudly and deep. And for so long that I hoped it had all been a cruel joke and waited for him to say 'fooled yer' so that I could get very angry. He knew what I was thinking.

'Nay! It's still true,' he said. 'Sorry. But I haven't yet learnt how to be sombre all the time. Some things still make me laugh. Sacrilegious isn't it? Confusing.'

I waited in the kitchen while Sonia made tea.

'What's all the laughing for?' she asked sourly, as though she'd expected our meeting to be a morbid occasion and was irritated to think that perhaps it was not and that she'd been in some way made a fool of by the laughter. It was difficult accounting for her mood; there was a time when we'd all been balmy friends, myself in the role of adopted son, a time when eighteen years between forty-eight and thirty seemed less than between sixty-six and forty-eight. I tried to chat but she sulked. It was strange and inexplicable.

Returning with the tray didn't wake Victor, who was dozing. The revelation had exhausted him, his body capitulated to the bed, jaw open and hanging from strain. I sat and waited. The coughing face had calmed to pale, his skin shiny like the handle of an often-held walking-stick. He snored. But as soon as he awoke he was bright.

'The first moments of waking are the best. Everything's forgotten, everything seems possible. After that – I remember.' I
handed him a cup of tea. 'And then everything becomes special.
Tea. I'm really tasting it now. Like when I gave up smoking.
Tastes come back. Now everything's coming back. Tastes,
colours, shapes – did you see the kitchen downstairs? Sonia's just
painted it white, as a surprise for me. Know how I knew it were
fresh done? Because the blue plates on the rack looked bluer.
Everything stands out. Everything's vivid. And everything has to
be special, too. Little things, like coffee, must be a certain taste,
not watery Nescafé but real – real beans. Or flowers in the house,
they have to smell, not your pretty dead things. But scented, as
nature intended. And food, must have food with its own flavours.
I get neurotic if cabbage tastes weedy, watery or the lamb gets
shredded like old shoelaces. Poor Sonia, she doesn't know what's
got into me.' He thought about that and couldn't resist bitterly
adding: 'Only I know what!' Then his mood switched again.
'Still, she thrives on it. *Thrives* on it!'

He sipped the tea gingerly. It was hot.

'But it's thinking that's the most difficult. Can't concentrate. I
try to work a thought through to the end but I can't concentrate.
Keep remembering. Get distracted.' He picked up a piece of
heavily fruited cake. 'Eat some. It's Sonia's. Yes, have to work
hard at thinking. But I win, in the end. I bloody do. All those
years of hard wage negotiations. Good training. Had to keep ten
moves ahead of those buggers, you know. But I'm jumping. I've
a lot to tell you, Maurice, and to talk about, and to show you. I
want to start at the beginning.' He drank more of his tea, dipped
the home-made fruit cake into the cup, sucked the juice and
began. This, more or less, is what he said:

'You're the first and only person I'm telling it to, and I know
you'll keep it to yourself if I ask it of you. About three years ago
I began to suffer from headaches and dizziness. It were in the

middle of the hospital workers' strike. Remember? Daft government policies. What a time *that* was. And I went at it full pelt, you know – bloody all night discussions about compromise, open-air gatherings up and down the country, executive committee meetings – the lot! And all on top of the daily routine demands of office and half the visiting foreign trade-union movement thrown at me to be looked after. So, blood-pressure I thought, and went for a check-up. The findings were that it was high, high but not pathological, and my general condition was good. No changes in the chest, heart O.K., and so on. I was relieved, you can imagine. Next day a phone call. Specialist's assistant. Would I go in and see them. Something had cropped up. They had to talk about it. I asked what it was, said I was desperately busy. No, she couldn't talk on the phone. I pressed to talk with the specialist who was also reluctant but I insisted. "There's a severe abnormality in the blood test," he said. I asked what it was. "A high white corpuscle count," he said. Just like that. "A high white corpuscle count," as though he were telling me I'd a bank overdraft. I can remember – there was a long silence on the phone.

'I thought, why is he telling me this over the phone? Then I remembered, I'd pressed him and I suppose he had to answer because I were a big and important trade-union leader and anyway it must be easier doing these things on the phone instead of having to face the person. Also I can be quite frightening down the wire sometimes. Funny how all these irrelevant thoughts were going through my mind. Anyway I arranged to go in the next day, and finished the conversation. And this is what was strange: I'd no sense of shock or fear, no sweating or increased pulse. Just a feeling of a great slowing down of time. Like I'd changed gear into slow motion. I vividly remember, I just do, I remember this one action, that I slowly, slowly turned my head around the room. Normally you'd jerk, quickly, your eye moving from one spot to another, but when I put that phone down my body movements had slow-owed down. I thought: you've only got a few months to live! And suddenly that seemed a whole lifetime.

'No, don't ask me to be logical about it. That's how I felt and so I'm telling you. Then – then came that heightened sensibility I told you of and with it' – Victor paused at this point as though uncertain how what he wanted to say would sound, or perhaps uncertain how it would be received, or even uncertain how to say it – 'and with it, with this heightened sensibility, came a great – a great increase of love. Or, if you like, a better sense of love. There was an overwhelming and completely non-sentimental love for my family, for Graeme and Hilda and for my grandson Jake. And especially for Sonia. I suddenly felt – well, filled with her spirit. I got a glimpse of my life as having been completely moulded to her expectations and abilities. Not regretfully, but gratefully. And then came a great feeling of relief. I was aware of how tired life had made me, how tired I was of myself and how now, now I could be held responsible for nothing more. Ever again. I was a dying man. And I remember feeling no fear of death, as though I understood it. It's true! I felt, how can I describe it, I felt – well I just felt a sensation of light and genuine, tranquil happiness and – curiosity!

'Yes! Me! Curiosity! Now I'd know, I thought. Now I'd get there and find out for myself. Ha! It was interesting! Suddenly dying seemed interesting. I sat there, in a state of shocked madness I suppose you'd call it, having this fantasy about rising before the Pearly Gates, and the answers I'd give. Can you imagine me? *Me*? Having such infantile dreams?

'Still, I don't suppose that mood stayed with me for more than about – oh, about two or three hours. No more. Because then this old grey matter began flowing.' He tapped his head. 'And then I said to myself: your Methodist childhood! It's creeping back. Watch out! You're hoping there's an after-life, a heaven. But there isn't. You've spent forty-five years reading the great doubters, the rationalists, the socialist philosophers and you know, you *know* there isn't. It's just that you're dying and you *want* there to be. Then it began. Not a conflict. No intellectual hijinks or torments of the soul. I just *felt*. I was full of just *feeling*. Low. Very low. I had to leave the office and come home. And I sat. The rest of the day just sat. Not thinking. Not working things out. There were no thought process. I were just – well – like fat with feeling. Feelings of complete and utter misery. Self-pity perhaps. And *that* were a new experience for me. I'd never indulged before. Never allowed myself emotional wallowings, you see. Sonia asked what it were and I told her it were the strike; but she'd seen me in strike times before, so I had to tell her half the truth, that I'd seen a doctor and he'd told me to go easy because of high blood pressure.

'Anyway, next day I went to see the specialist. He said: "We're not certain but all the evidence points to myloid leukaemia." I knew the implications of that of course but I waited to hear it spelt out. "Fifty per cent of the people in your condition live for three years," he said. "Of the other fifty per cent, many live for five, some for ten. A few have been known to live for twenty but that's rare. Some have died within the year but that's just as rare. You have my answer." Ha! Yes, I had his answer all right. But as you said, they can be wrong. You're right, it's been known. So I saw someone else.

'And what a bastard he turned out to be. A diehard old Tory who'd obviously always hated my guts. When I asked him for a prognosis he said: "If you've got some papers that need signing you can leave them. If you've got a fortune to make I'd start making it right now." I bit my tongue on that one and just asked about the possibility of cure or spontaneous recovery. And you know what he said? "Cure is a dirty word!" A right bastard he were.

'It was from my own doctor, my own old G.P., that I managed

to find a little comfort. I remember he embraced me first and then said: "Vic, you aren't worried about it are you? *You're* not going to die of leukaemia. A heart attack, maybe, a plane crash, anything! But not leukaemia. Myloid leukaemia", he said, "for a person in your condition and at your age is a benign ailment. Eat very well. Go to bed early. Get up a bit later. Avoid infections. Keep outdoors as much as possible, and – don't tell anybody, it only creates the wrong atmosphere." Great man, that. Restored my sanity.

'So – there it is. I belonged to the fifty per cent who last three years. My time's up. The Myleran and Purinethol are having less and less effect. I'm up and I'm down. I recover but I recover more slowly. It still just looks like high blood-pressure to Sonia but *I* know. I *know* what's happening.'

He wanted to carry on but he was grey, as though ashes from a doused fire had settled on him. The life force seemed drained away. I stood up, anxious. He flagged me reassuringly. 'It's all right, just a turn. I'll be all right after a sleep. But you'd better go. Come again soon. Tomorrow, the day after. Leave the bloody students. Attend to me. I really need you, Maurice, lad. And I've things to show you. But don't, I beg you, don't tell Sonia.'

My most difficult moment was passing her in order to get out of the house. She seemed to be waiting to see in what state I'd be, her eyes not reluctant to show greed for information. It was unnerving. I fled with excuses of being late for a tutorial and made an obscene, hurried joke about how well Victor was and how this reflected on her caring of him, which should have worked but didn't. She saw me out of the house with fury and I understood none of it.

I came again three days later. Victor was in his bedroom sitting at a table near to an open window and looking very much in control of himself, surprisingly so. Once again it was that bright and sunny day to make everything and everybody sparkle. He was in pyjamas and dressing-gown, freshly washed and ironed, like his ruddy face soft and clear from a hot bath and close shave. The bed was meticulously laid out and folded with dazzling white sheets and an abundance of starched pillows. The smell in the room was a mixture of lavender polish from within and new-mown grass from without where Sonia was cutting their pocket-sized lawn. A good old working-class atmosphere of scrubbed and clean prettiness: dust would not be found even over the curtain pelmet.

'Look at her!' said the waning campaigner, 'can't keep still. You watch her and you'll see: she must always be doing something.' He caught me admiring the neat room with its laid out bed of blinding sheets. 'See those pressed sheets and pillows? That's what you call being looked after. Not a crease or a wrinkle in them. Know why? She changes them every day. Believe it or not I get into fresh sheets every night. I tell her there's no need but she takes no notice. "You spent good money on a washing machine," she says, "I'll use it then." Love it, of course. Always did! Friday nights we usually had a change of bedding and that were always a special night. But now? Every night's special!' He smiled as he nodded towards the crisp, white arrangement of linen. And then added, in his best negotiating, intimate voice: 'Oh, by the way, Maurice, I've told Sonia you're doing the rounds of the galleries for me and that's why you're going to have to keep coming. A little lie, but you don't mind do you, lad? Want some coffee? I'll see to coffee and you read this.'

He handed me a letter. 'That letter is one of the things I want to talk to you about.' He shuffled out. 'Came two days before you saw me last.' I looked at the blue sheet of large handwriting. It was almost a child's scrawl. There was no address at the top of the page, no date, and no endearing beginning. Simply:

I was thinking the other day. I used never to be able to call you darling. Do you remember? When we first met I was really plain. Plain-minded I mean, not looking. I was pretty looking but I felt daft saying darling and sweetheart and those things. Took about two years before I could bring myself to call you any but your name. And I only ever gave in because you bullied me. Got proper annoyed in fact. You *made* me say the word, forced me. Remember? I do. It was after we'd been to have tea with my grandmother. A Sunday afternoon. One of those big spreads. Everything thrown on the table, you know, from home-made pickled onions to thick old crusty rhubarb pies. And she was making her usual fuss of me. Adored me she did and I did her too, and she was teasing me and saying 'she's a little darling, isn't she a little darling, she's my little darling.' And when we walked home you turned on me and said 'she can say the word why can't you?' 'What word?' I asked. 'Darling!' You yelled. 'Go on, say it!' You did look funny, your face all angry while your mouth was saying words of loving. Didn't go together somehow. 'SAY DARLING' you shouted at me and that made me giggle. And the more I giggled the more angry you got. But you won. You made me say it. Darling! Sweetheart Victor, dearest Victor, darling Victor, darling, darling and my heart. I was remembering. Just today. For no reason. While I was outside cleaning the windows.

There was no signature at the bottom of the page.

Victor came in with a tray of coffee and tarts smelling freshly of dough straight from the oven.

'Sonia?' I asked, referring to the letter.

'Sonia,' he replied, handing me an envelope. 'Came in this, with the rest of the post, fully stamped. Posted from our own post office at the bottom of the road and written, presumably, in the downstairs lounge while I was upstairs in the bedroom.'

'Have you spoken to her about it?'

'No. Nor she to me. Doesn't even behave as though something were up. We both ignore it. And I suppose I'd've forgotten it if this hadn't arrived.' He handed me another envelope containing the same blue paper and written upon in the same large handwriting. Again, it had been addressed, stamped and posted. 'Came this morning. She always sandwiches it between the rest of the mail and, like the other, no traditional beginning or ending.' I read:

You used to tease me about God. Soft brain I had in them days. Could I help it though? My soft brain yes but not my religiousness, that were my upbringing. No one can be blamed for that, though they do say the sins of the fathers shall fall upon the sons but that's cruel and unreasonable. Not that you were like that, you weren't cruel and unreasonable no never I'm not saying that. But you teased and you shouldn't have done because I was very hurt by it. You didn't know that I was. Very hurt. To begin with. Then my brain got hard. 'God is one man's invention to frighten other men into being good,' you said. 'But no one's good if they're frightened.' That's what you said and it sounded very reasonable to me. Besides, there was the war and all of them soldiers being gassed and slaughtered and then it happened to my brother Stan so I couldn't much believe in God. But I missed him. I don't mind telling you I missed God. Used to give me lovely pictures to think about. It was a long time before I knew what it was you gave me. Better. You know that don't you? After the teasing and tormenting my brain got harder and I grew proud of what I got to understand and how I could listen to you and your mates arguing and saving the world and make up my own mind. Did you know I grew? Couldn't talk or argue much

or write but I grew from God to you. Became a woman.
For a while at least.

That was all.

'Well?' my perplexed friend asked, 'what do you make of it?
I don't think she's written more than a hundred letters in her life
and most of them were postcards or anyway just a handful of
phrases.'

'I don't know,' I said. 'Does she suspect that you're – ' I
couldn't bring myself to say the word.

'Dying?' Victor said it for me and answered, 'no, I don't
think so. And anyway, so what? Why can't she just talk to me?
Or at least bring me them up as notes and say, "I've just jotted
down a few thoughts which I'd like you to read?" I mean we're
not quarrelling, there's no silent battle between us. We're great
friends in fact. In fact,' he blushed and smiled at his blush, 'in fact,
don't laugh, we're lovers again. Grotesque isn't it? I mean look
at us, I've got a sixty-six year old belly on me and she's got grey
hairs growing out from her chin.'

We moved on. Drank coffee and talked about Victor's book
on art to which he'd added another page. 'I won't ever finish it,'
he said, 'too much bloody reading and research to do and my
brain can't cope with it now. But doodling, I'm doodling and it
keeps me occupied.'

It was another fortnight before commitments allowed me to
visit Victor again. He rang me up one evening in a depressed
state and so railed at me for neglecting 'your best friend', that I
cancelled the next morning's tutorial and came to see him. It was
a gloomy sky and he'd drawn the curtains.

'Can't bear heavy skies. Sooner imagine it was night time than
face morbid bloody clouds.'

He lay propped up against those starched, over-fed cushions.
There were half-a-dozen around him now as though they'd

reproduced themselves. The atmosphere of the house was irritability.

Sonia greeted me at the door with a vicious 'you again?' and asked, no, *ordered* me to wait before going up. I followed her into the kitchen. She was preparing a mid-morning coffee snack for Victor and banged another cup and saucer on to the tray for me. I thought that was all and reached to take it. 'Wait!' she snapped. From out the oven she pulled a platter of scones, prised off four, sliced them in half, opened the fridge, took out a bowl of double-whipped cream, some of which she scooped up and spread over the four halves of scone, returned the bowl, bent down to a cup-board – I noticed she didn't bend her legs but seemed able to simply fold in half without effort – bent down to a cupboard for some strawberry jam, which she dripped over the cream, and only then handed me the tray.

'Have you been quarrelling?' I asked Victor.

'We never quarrel,' he replied, picking up the cream-flushed scone as though it were evidence, 'we only ever sulk.'

'Well she's sulking, why?' I'd not enjoyed her curtness.

'Would you believe it, she wants me to get out of bed, pack a case and go with her for a week to Mytholmroyd on the Moors where we used to court. Isn't that daft? Now *that's* a daft thing for you.'

Two very distinct Sonias were emerging: Victor's Sonia, the one she showed to him, and ours. I had lost patience with what had been left over for the rest of us, but was beginning to like his.

'What's daft about it?' I asked.

'Doesn't she know I'm bloody dy ... ' He snatched the word from his mouth. 'No, she doesn't, poor bitch.' Victor began a small sigh; but such was his unhappiness that it grew, despite him, to a gasp, a profound clutching for air. 'It's no good, Maurice, I can't take it. I thought I had it in me. But I haven't. I'm frightened. So frightened and unhappy. You think: surely something will happen, someone ... a discovery in time. Something always did, didn't it? For all our mistakes, whenever we made fools of ourselves or got ill there were help, a cure, forgiveness. I can't really be dying! That's just plain silly. What? All this gone, stopped, done? But it is. Nothing will help. I know it now. And it's such a – such a – burden, such a heavy, rotten burden, this knowledge. It's not only the gloom, the melancholy, it's the self-pity, the nostalgia, the frustration. I feel so humiliated lying here and watching myself become frightened. No one should have to know it. It's not fair. A man's not made to live with such a knowledge. Look at it!' He flung his arms at everything around him: the bits and pieces of art, his books, the food, even the glowering outside. 'Love it!' he said, on the verge of tears. 'I love it, love it! I just plainly and simply love it.'

It was the only time I was to see him cry. It didn't last long.

'Bloody Christ! don't let her see me like this. There'd be hell to pay. Murder me she would.' At which he laughed, with great release, enormous laughter until he was puffed out and I had the chance to change the subject. I asked him had he written any more towards his book.

'No, Maurice, lad,' he cooed, the Yorkshire brogue surfacing to help bury his emotional lapse. 'No, but I make notes, I make notes, you know, soft bloody things, on scraps here and there.'

'What notes?' I persisted in case he should evade me.

'Oh, nought of importance. Look!' he drew out a sheet, a typed circular I think it was, from between the leaves of a large book of paintings by Giotto. He'd written on the back of it.

There are the oppressors and the victims. From this come many questions: why does a man oppress and why does another allow himself to become a victim? Also: does the man who oppresses know he's an oppressor? Does the victim know he's a victim? Or are there two kinds of oppressor and victim – those who know what they are and those who don't. Does one man say I enjoy oppressing and another say this is not oppression but a necessary force for this reason or that? Do oppressors *always* have explanations for their actions?

When I looked up Victor was searching me for confirmation of his own contempt: 'Isn't that a mess?' I didn't protest. It was. 'When I wrote that down I thought it was the beginning of a profound inquiry that would unravel why everyone concludes it's a rotten life. Have you noticed that? Everyone says it's a rotten life, "people are rotten!", life and literature, all filled with characters whose experience of the world is depressing. So – who upsets them? Speak to the man who they say has upset them and you find *he also* thinks the world is a rotten place and that people are rotten. And who's upset *him*? Where does it begin? Everyone knows it's a terrible life only it never seems possible to lay your finger on the culprit, the cause. I know people have got answers – religious, political, philosophic. But at the end of everyone's life, whether he's a revolutionary, a dictator, a pope, a millionaire, a worker, a prime minister, a socialist citizen, a citizen of the West, a great artist, a great scientist, a great philosopher – for all of them! Terrible life! By the end of it they're all weary and dis-illusioned and dispirited.

'I mean, listen to this.' He reached for a small, olive-green leather book. 'Ruskin wrote *Modern Painters* in 1843, when he was twenty-four years old – twenty-four! Ha! Thirty-one years later some lady friend of his – er – ' he flicked to the front of the book ' – the "Younger Lady of the Thwaite, Coniston", she makes a selection from the book and he adds footnotes here and there, and here's one of them, now listen:

"I forget, now, what I meant by 'liberty' in this passage; but I often used the word in my first writings, in a good

sense, thinking of Scott's moorland rambles and the like.
It is very wonderful to me, now, to see what hopes I had
once: but Turner was alive then, and the sun used to shine,
and the rivers to sparkle."

'So! What's the malaise? The central illness running through it
all? If I'm to write a book on art I should have opinions on these
things. But I haven't. I've been a trade-union leader too long.
Should've given up at forty and started to study. Or even fifty or
fifty-five. Wasn't too late then, but now? Not now, Maurice lad,
even with your help.'

He'd relieved but tired himself out. I lingered on a little while
giving him my own gossip and then left. There'd not been
another letter from Sonia.

I'd planned to visit him again in ten days but was asked at the
last moment to undertake a fortnight's lecture tour of the States,
in place of a colleague who'd gone down with an ignored and
festering appendix. Victor was bitterly disappointed when I spoke
to him on the phone. 'Don't neglect me, Maurice, don't forget
your old friend will you?' I told him not to be an idiot and that it
was insulting if, even for a second, he considered I might. 'I
knoa, I knoa.' He always moved into a heavy dialect at such
moments. 'Listen,' he whispered into the phone, 'I've had another
letter. I'll send it you. Read on the plane. Sssh! No more. She's
coming.'

I read the letter on receiving it and once more in the plane.
Again it had been posted and again there was no formal beginning or ending, just an undated note.

The only time I ever swore was a night you got more than
normal drunk and wept because things weren't going right
in the union and you began complaining at me. You told
me, 'You don't care about me or my state or the fact that I'm
losing me nerve and failing me mates, do you? And you

haven't a care for rights nor conditions nor wages nor nothing.' Remember that? How you raged and wept and screamed? 'I'm going to pieces I'm going to pieces and you don't care and you don't understand.' Very loud you were that night my love and I railed back, 'Of course I care of course I understand but I won't give consolations to a man when he's filled with pity and shit. That's what you are,' I said. 'You're filled with pity and shit.' Ha! The only time you wept and I swore that was. And that *was* a tense time. Very tense time that was my love. I'm laughing as I write it down. You looked so funny so startled. I felt very bucked with myself to have startled you so. It was serious then but I confess now I giggled afterwards. Went away and giggled to myself. I'm laughing even as I write about it. Oh dear. Ha! ha! Full of pity and shit I said. You forgot all about your going to pieces then. Aye. You were so shocked. Pity and shit! Ha! ha!

As soon as I returned from the States I visited Victor. He was in a glassy-eyed cold mood. 'You could find the time then could you?'

I ignored his sarcasm and tried to restore his spirits by giving him a present of a sketch I'd bought. 'Found it in a little junk shop in New Bedford.' I watched him, anxious to catch a sign of pleasure. 'Now, look at it carefully. What's the signature?' He peered, reached for his glasses and peered again.

'John Rushton? Who's Rushton?'

'Are you sure it says Rushton?' I asked, 'that's what *I* thought, but look again.' He looked again.

'Rushton. It says Rushton. That's all I can see,' and testily handed back the sketch.

'What about Ruskin?' I whispered to give the suggestion its fullest drama.

'*Ruskin*?' He snatched back the drawing. Ruskin was his

mentor and Victor had always said how, of all possessions, he coveted a Ruskin drawing no matter how modest.

Now he pushed his spectacles up and down his nose trying to focus and refocus them into a clearer remagnification. They were not strong enough. He moved to a drawer and pulled out a huge magnifying glass. I'd not seen him so excited for a long time.

'My God! It could be. It just could be. Now isn't that a thrill!' Indeed it was to see him so joyous. He sat back in his brown old granny armchair. 'That's revived me no end that has. You're a lovely friend. Forgive my jadedness, I mean – a Ruskin! Well!' He seemed exhausted at the thought.

'Ah, Maurice, there's no doubt about it the soul depends on the body.' He began breathing upon and wiping the magnifying glass. 'It's not been a good period while you've been away. Not good at all. I've started trying to imagine this other place again. I mean supposing it *did* exist, just supposing. What *could* it be like? Not like the paintings that's for sure, with beatific angels and grateful new arrivals looking holy but, I don't know – could it be somewhere where we all are as we were except that the tense edge is taken out of relationships? You know, no competing to be one up on the next man, no pride in brilliance, no urgency to be proven wise or correct, no malice for being less intelligent? No! that sounds dull, unappealing. Ha! A man's vibrant when he's all *that*, isn't he?' He was walking around the room, his restless movements echoing a restless mind.

'I mean I can't even begin to imagine what it would be like *visually*. Where do you *place* it, this after-life? And then I think: it's not a physical place, Victor, that's where you go wrong. It's a spiritual state, a state of awareness unconfined by a physical framework. Ha! And so I lie here trying to project myself into "a spiritual state of awareness unconfined by a physical framework". Ever tried to do that? Try it some day. And then I get angry and I say to myself: "Darkness! Nothing! When you're dead that's it. Over! Done! If you want satisfaction, Victor lad, then look to your life, your political battles, the fights you fought for other men." But who can do that for long? Who can dwell on his past and go scratching around for bits of victory? Eh? A smug man, perhaps. But I'm not a smug man, Maurice, never was. So what's left? No after-life I can conceive of and no past to feel at peace with. And I go round and round in circles driving myself mad because even the very act of contemplating it, me! thinking about whether there's a heaven, another life, the very worrying about such things makes me feel guilty and shabby. "You, Victor? Worrying about where you're going? Frightened are you?" I taunt myself. "Frightened?" I mock. "Poor, feeble-minded man, you. You who used to be so confident about it all beginning with birth and ending with death. You! Want a comfortable little heaven to go to now? Do you?" And I'm a merciless bugger you know. Really get to the heart of myself, where it hurts. Always been like that. Have you ever thought about the tone of voice your conscience has? They're all different you know. Every one's got a conscience talks to them in a different tone of voice. Mine jeers. Very acidly.'

He looked again at the drawing. It was of a viaduct spanning two rocky hills between which a fast river fell over other rock formations. The time of day seemed early morning when mists curl through valleys and desperately cling where they can before the sun takes them in its first deep breath. A typical Ruskin setting in which he could explore his favourite loves: architecture and the elements of rock, water and cloud.

'A Ruskin,' Victor murmured. 'What do you know.'

There was a knock on the door. It was Sonia. She stood, massively, facing the door's edge and looking down at the floor as though, like the maid in the house, she had discreetly to avoid confronting a private scene. I noticed for the first time she did indeed have hair on her chin. Ignoring me completely she addressed herself sternly to Victor: 'You haven't forgotten?'

'Noa, noa, lass,' Victor said and, when she'd gone, 'you wouldn't believe it but when there's no one in the house she's a changed woman. Becomes visibly younger, playful and tender. You know how it is when some people are angry, they turn – well – ugly. Their face collapses. Get defeated by their own irritation. *Not*, mind you, to be confused with outrage which makes some people magnificent. Well that's how it is with her. When people are in the house she's mean and irritable, becomes heavy, vicious, even treats *me* like a stranger. When they leave she's full of outrage and she's magnificent. Even that massive bulk of hers moves elegantly. Now she's heavy as a landslide because a gaggle of old colleagues are due in half an hour – God knows what for.'

'Is that my hint to go?' I asked.

'Good God, no! Just wait downstairs while I change. I'm not letting *that* lot see me in bedclothes.'

I dreaded hovering around downstairs, it would be very icy there. Then I thought – hell! I've known Sonia nearly fifteen years and whatever else she might resent in whoever else, she had no cause to resent me. Besides, it was selfish to surround Victor with unpleasantness now.

She was ironing in the kitchen. I stood in the doorway, feeling for the right tone and the right words. She tolerated my presence for a few seconds.

'There are chairs in the front room,' she said.

'Stop it, Sonia, for Christ's sake!' The deliberate rudeness of her voice made me angry. 'It's not an easy world and I'm far from being the most perfect of men but *you've* been given no cause to be so unfriendly.' She thumped the iron down on each new crease but said nothing. 'Even if only because your husband needs our friendship you ought to show more grace.' She continued ironing with such resolute uncommunicativeness that I abruptly decided it was best to abandon her presence. She had her reasons for hostility and whether justified or not it seemed futile to seek explanations for them. I retreated.

The front room reflected, in a way I'd not noticed until now, their two distinct personalities. The wallpaper was obviously Sonia's choice. A pattern of yellow flowers with the flourish of nature's energy but none of its vitality. The kind of design which conned a large market into believing it had purchased floral elegance. Not that Sonia had a weakness for superficial refinements, no, it had probably been the bright colour that attracted *her*, its cleanness, its scrubbed prettiness. There were curtains to match and even furniture upholstered in the same material. That part of the room was fussy, over-protected, you felt you were not welcome to sit there because it feared you besmirching it.

On the other hand there were some choice pieces of furniture, nothing precious, but used and loved, like the Georgian glass cabinet and the Victorian roll-top desk, and the huge knobbly Windsor chair, an early one, nicely warped by fickle temperatures and with a seat shining from the shifting, no doubt, of fickle temperaments. The plain and framed Victorian weaving of flowers was hers, the modern prints were his; the highly polished brass and copper were hers, the pieces of sculpture his. Even the glass cabinet contained two tastes: the porcelain was Victor's and the sea-side miniatures, now prized by some collectors in pursuit of nostalgia at the price of ugliness, were Sonia's – only *her* nostalgia was real: each item was a cherished holiday.

And so it was with the whole room, everything could be pointed to and guessed to be his or hers and yet – what bound both tastes so that each sat at peace with the other? It took me some time to discover, but suddenly I realized what it was: every item, chosen by no matter whom, had been chosen because the owner had cared deeply for it for one reason or another: aesthetics or emotion, tastes or association. And so a strange harmony pervaded in which every piece seemed, with grace, to acknowledge and permit the other's existence. It affected me pleasantly: with relief I discovered myself unable to remain angry over Sonia's rudeness, at which moment I sat down, weary, in the dark-stained Windsor chair, which I also discovered swivelled, and swivelled myself round and round in front of the roll-top desk until my eye caught a familiar sheet of blue paper. It was another of Sonia's letters, one not yet sent and innocently left lying around.

The lilac's dead. Don't ask me how but it's had a blight. Remember the lilac? We planted it forty-one years ago and uprooted it four times for four changes of house. It survived all those uprootings and now ... I'd be lost without my garden. It's not just a place I potter around in you know. I think you think it is. 'Thank God she's occupied,' you say to yourself. I bet. No, it's a place where I think my best thoughts. My only thoughts in fact even though they don't amount to many. And where I touch all manner of things like earth and leaves and squashed worms and stones and colours and fresh air and smells and winds and clouds and rain and sunlight and the cycle of things. You used to be like that, loving the cycle of things. It's you I got it from. Remember how the lilac came? You brought it home one day and said we must start a garden. You'd got it from the old railway porter. It was a sucker you told me, lilac cuttings were always suckers, from the roots not the branch. A thin thing it was with only a few whispery strands between living and dying. I didn't think it would take but you did and it started our garden off. What about those arguments we had? We had our first rows over our first garden. What shape it should be what should grow in it which way it should face. You would insist the sun came up in one place while I knew darn well it came up in another.

So what did we do? Daft buggers we set the alarm to get
up before sunrise. You were wrong of course. You've no
idea how important it was to me to have been right about
that. It was my first landmark. Gave me great confidence
that did. And as for the quarrels about what we should grow
well – I thought it would end our marriage. I wanted more
vegies and you wanted more flowers. You said it wasn't
a real saving to grow our own vegies, only an illusion. But
you said all right we'll have more vegies only I had to keep
accounts. You made me work out what it cost in seed and
labour and I had to weigh all what grew and then check it
with the price in markets and make a sum of it all. And I
did it too. Worked all hours figuring it out. Mad people.
But I loved it. Columns of figures all very neat, and grand
headings. Looked very important. I got top marks at school
for neatness. Loved it. And was I proud. I *was* proud. Gave
me great pleasure and I was right. Again. It *did* pay to grow
our own vegies. That was my second landmark. A huge
garden. Planted everything in it bar the sun. When you
insisted I learn to drive a car, that was a landmark. When
you asked me to show the Italian delegation round London
without you that was a landmark. When you first went
abroad for a fortnight and I carried my affairs and your
affairs alone without you that was a landmark. When you
first put your head between my legs that was a landmark.

The shock of the last intimacy made me shoot up and move
quickly to the window as though pretending even to myself I'd
been there all along. A hot flush had risen to my cheeks.

At the same moment the house moved into action. The union
men knocked at the front door, Sonia loomed with a tray of
coffee and home-made chocolate cake. Victor came downstairs.
I'd not seen him in clothes for a long time, the effect was shatter-

ing. They hung uncomfortably, pointlessly, as though on an alien body, a thin and pale body. He was wearing a light-brown check suit, a complete outfit with waistcoat and tie as though determined to show he was still very much in the business of living. The effort boomeranged: he looked the dying man he so wanted not to appear, and it forced both Sonia and I to register his condition with shock. The shock cemented us together. She surmounted hers sooner than I did mine and moved out of the room. Then Victor and I exchanged glances: had she understood? We couldn't be certain. She'd pretended very well. I felt a spiritual double-agent, in collusion with them both.

The men were from the executive of his old union. They'd come to ask if he'd permit a new headquarters to be named after him and would he open it in nine months' time. 'I'm fundamentally opposed to a building being named after anyone.' His seriousness was worrying. Then he grinned: 'But I'd love to see myself made an exception of.' They were delighted. 'On one condition,' he returned to his mischievous seriousness, 'that you assure and promise me a sum of money will be set aside for purchasing the paintings and prints of young artists to go on the walls. You've known it's been my passion to help young painters and civilize you barbarians.'

His performance was a joy. Like a sensitive political geiger-counter he could squeeze between stubbornness, prejudice and the bloody-mindedness for which he knew, and complained, trades union leaders were infamous. With charm and a blunt commonsense – edged golden from dippings into the glitter of art – he could make groups and individuals do just what he wanted. It was a huge power and he'd been loved by the rank and file for not abusing it, though dreaded by the hierarchy, who never allowed him to leave the industrial arena since he could not be relied upon to pursue the 'practical deceits of politics'.

The encounter tired him but none of his old comrades could

see that. He seemed able to will the blood into his face till they left after which he caved in, ashen, and Sonia stormed, as though I wasn't there: 'That's what they did always. Drained you! Selfish men! You only ever surrounded yourself with selfish men who used you, built their careers on you and then left you. Selfish men!' She seemed to be calling after them hoping they'd hear her as they walked down the road: 'SELFISH MEN!'

It became necessary for us to help Victor upstairs. When he'd reached the bed he was puffing helplessly. Sonia looked at me, not so hostile now but pleading with me to leave. Of course I should have gone and invented the excuse of an imminent appointment but Victor wanted me to stay, and bargained: 'Help me undress and then you can go. Ten minutes. What's ten minutes to you?'

He'd been the dignified leader in front of his ex-colleagues but now, vulnerable through exhaustion, he abandoned himself to begging favours. I looked at Sonia to get her approval. She gave it. Once alone he chattered as I pulled, with scant aid from him, the clothes off his back. His eyes were closed as he talked.

'She's always been like that. Anxious about abuse. Me, I never worry. Hell! It was a lonely life. In order to find one friend you had to let dozens abuse you I reckoned. Not her though. I always took it easy, she always scowled. Let the lads come I always said, they ate a little, drank, lingered; *my* family's atmosphere was like that – open house. Not hers though. Give everything to the friends she loved, but *everything*. Mean as old socks to the rest.'

By the time I left him he was almost asleep. Downstairs, Sonia, for the first time in years, kissed me goodbye. An unspoken conspiracy began. Not one where I revealed knowledge of her strange letters, or betrayed even the tiniest hint about Victor's illness, but a pact where both seemed to agree that he was now unable to gauge for himself how much rest he should take. Besides, I was convinced she had understood the terrible portents.

And he did need protection. As I was entering the house on

my next visit a young man passed me wearing a bright, confident smile and clothes aspiring to a colourfully 'pop' gaiety, made bloodless by suburban tailoring. He seemed pumped up by his meeting with Victor who, no doubt, I would find deflated. Sonia, her scowls now entirely devoted to others than me, grimaced and mocked at this cock's breezy farewell.

'Now watch him go back and say to them, "Well I had a word with old Vic and he agreed with me that your balls *ought* to be painted black!" Bloody little opportunist! Here, take this up with you.'

She thrust the tray into my hands.

'Do you have to do this all day?' I asked.

'Never mind', she nodded, and gave strange blinks in the direction of the up-and-coming young unioncrat, 'never mind, it's going to stop soon, mark me. I'll find ways of scaring the buggers off, see if I don't. They'll know the entrance fee for bleeding Gods white!'

Spread out on the kitchen table were old newspapers and on them her beloved collection of copper and brass. It was metal-cleaning hour. She massaged her hands back into rubber gloves and returned to her polishing and mumbling.

Victor was at his desk. He was not deflated, just irritated. His glasses were pushed back on a head stooped forward and peering at the 'Ruskin' sketch through an even bigger magnifying glass.

'My bloody eyesight's going. They told me that would go. Jesus Christ! I just have to sit here and watch myself disintegrate. But you know what, Maurice, I think it *is* a Ruskin. Look, compare it with this facsimile of his signature. It's shakier than the other that's all, mine's an early sketch, but ... '

It was true. The facsimile was an old man's handwriting, the drawing's signature was firm and confident but the similarity was unmistakable. Said Victor: 'How in hell did it get to New Bedford I wonder? Now there's a story for someone. What lives were

wrapped around the voyage of that, eh? The history of a whole
age there.'

I asked who was the parting guest.

'A young "father" from one of the printing chapels.' He was
grumpy to have to think about it again. 'They want to come out
on a token sympathy strike with the footplate men. You know
what the real problem is of industrial relations? To sort out the
true militants from the holiday-makers. There's a lot of *them*.' I
poured out the tea which he sipped with a noisy relish. 'And
they're bullies with it, cheap Chicago-style mobsters. I said to
him: "While you're on strike, losing your week's wages", which
they can ill-bloody-afford, "while you're being loyal and com-
radely and losing your wages," I said, "do you know where
R.S.B. is?" He's their General Secretary. "No," he said, "where?"
"In the bloody Canary Islands having a holiday," I said, "buying
a house for himself out of union funds for when he retires." And
d'you know what this young fellow did? You won't believe it –
he grinned! He grinned and he nudged me and he said: "Now
isn't that just like R.S.B.!" Admired it! He admired his union
boss being like all the employers so's to show they could screw
their way into power and affluence same as them! Doesn't that
depress you? Depresses the hell out of me. Can't win now,
Maurice, capitalism's built up a resistance to criticism. Like
certain diseases, all the known antibiotics can't touch them. The
virus laughs back at us, look, fat and greedy.'

He picked up the sketch to look at it again, as though unable to
believe that here was a sheet of paper that once lay virgin in front
of, and to be filled by, a man he counted among the great minds
of the nineteenth century.

'He'd've been depressed. Wonder what he'd have said though,
what new distinctions he'd have carved out to illuminate the mess.'

There was something off-key about the way Victor was
speaking. From the moment I'd entered the room his tone of voice

had had that kind of heartiness the guilty assume to soften impending and unpleasant confessions. But he was not yet ready to confess.

'You know what the attractive quality was about the aristocracy? Their sensitivity. Oh not all of them, *I* know that. Some right hard bastards among them, I *know* that. But generally speaking. Sensitivity! Came from good-breeding, long familiarity with the best. And so *they* had the confidence to doubt themselves occasionally, be self-critical. Not this Prime Minister though. Vicious, stubborn, tart and middle-class he is. Mustn't ever be wrong, oh no! The virus is a Prime Minister with a smug smile who plays the organ, speaks French like a first-year at comprehensive, and we've got no antibiotics. Hurts. What a mess, eh? What a waste! What a life!'

He cleaned the drips of tea off his moustache. 'Would you get the Ruskin framed for me?' he asked. I said of course. We sipped in silence. For both of us our focal point was the bed. When we weren't chatting we stared, dazzled by the lovely linen of the high-stacked white pillows.

'I mean,' said Victor, 'sometimes I feel guilty for dozing on it of an afternoon. I fear she might come up and change it *twice* a day.'

There was something desultory about the way he was now speaking that made me guess the announcement could be held back no longer.

'They want me in hospital.' He tossed it to me grudgingly as though chagrined. I knew something was waiting to be said. 'A few days, week maybe, for preliminary tests, you know the sort of thing. Think they may have found a new drug.' He didn't sound convinced but I was immediately alive with enthusiasms about the extraordinary achievements of medicine. Maybe there was something in it. He squinted at me from the edge of his tea cup and crept out of his scepticism. 'Think so?' he allowed himself to believe my hymns to the endless brilliance of scientists. 'Well', he conceded, 'I could more easily bring myself to believe in the possibility of a cure than the possibility of an after-life.'

'Are you still dwelling on those morbid prospects?' Suddenly light-hearted, I felt able to admonish him. And why not? After D.N.A. what *really* is impossible for those sweet madmen in their underfinanced laboratories?

'Even if I'm cured, Maurice, lad,' said Victor, 'it won't ever stop me thinking about the after-death. Not now. I'd've been too near it to leave off contemplating now. Here,' he handed me some blue envelopes, 'two arrived in one day. How about that? She wrote one, sealed the envelope, wrote another and *didn't* open the first to put them together, no! posted them separately! Do you think something's wrong in *her* blood also?'

On the day we got married I thought you hated me. I must tell you that because it's the only time I've seen hate in your eyes. What am I doing marrying a man who hates me I thought to myself? You were so silent so angry. But after-wards well I didn't ever say but I used never to be able to take my eyes off you. No one had ever been so tender *and* so certain. And you used to sing. Once a visitor came from abroad I can't remember where, France I think, and he said to me, 'Good God there's someone who can still sing.' Our first son sang also. I remember we'd wake and find him standing up by his cot looking down on us, not crying, not murmuring, nor nothing, just patiently waiting for us to wake up. And when we did he was the first thing we looked at and he knew it and waited for it and then gave us a slow smile and started to hum. Nearly every morning was like that. You were daft about him. Wanted him to be a com-poser. You used to play classical records in the bedroom while he was asleep. 'It's best it sinks into him uncon -

sciously,' you said. Weird theories you had. You wouldn't
ever *tell* him to think of music as a career, that would put
him off, but if it went in subliminally (do you know I
couldn't remember that word blessed if I could but I knew
you'd said something like that and I've just spent a whole
hour looking through the dictionary for it. Lots of lovely
words in the dictionary but I can't remember them. Did
you know a siderite was a steel-coloured stone? That to
sibilate was to hiss? That a solatium was a sum of money
paid for injured feelings? And solazzi was a stick of liquorice? And that liquorice is not lickerish as I've always called
it, no it's to be good like a cook at preparing dainties only
they stopped using that word in 1600 and started to use the
word lickerous). There! see what writing to you does for
me? Where was I? Music. There was one day, my God
don't I remember that day, the children must've been about
nine and eleven and you took us up a climb on the Peaks.
Dangerous old route you took us. *You* were scared too.
You won't remember it but you got us on to a tricky part
where you had to go back and forwards across a gap four
times in order to help me and the children and you were
sweating. The children thought it was great fun. They
would. You never let them be frightened of anything. Not
always a good thing I thought. Still, I remember that trip
for three reasons. The dangerous climb was one. The other
was you letting out by accident that you'd had a girl friend
before me who'd climbed with you on that same walk. You
blushed when you realized it'd been let out. In fact I wasn't
sure if you were talking about a girl-friend before me or
*after* me ... And the third thing was the song we sang at the
top when we got there. We ate the sandwiches and there
was a big wind and you cried out like a madman 'we must
sing against the wind. Good for the lungs and the spirit.' So

you taught us a round. The words were

> By the waters the waters of Babylon
> We lay down and wept and wept
> For these I am
> Thee remember thee remember thee remember
> These I am.

What did it mean? I never knew what it meant. Not all this time. 'We wept for these I am.' What are 'these I am'? Do you think you got it wrong? We all used to get songs wrong as children. I used to think it was 'Good King Wences last looked out' instead of 'Good King Wenceslas looked out.' Perhaps it should have been 'thee Zion.' Perhaps we should have wept for thee Zion. Or no, now I come to think of it you were probably right after all and we wept because I am these things, we are these things, all are these things.

When I looked up Victor said: 'I could only recall the hair-raising climb. Nothing else.' Then, as I turned to read the second letter I remembered: he wasn't going to show me the letter I'd read, uninvited, while waiting downstairs some weeks ago. Or perhaps Sonia had decided not to send it. And were there others she'd written and not sent? After all, they were developing in fluency and it was obvious she obtained great pleasure composing them.

I want you to start making plans for the future. It struck me. Just like that. Well not really just like that. In fact I was looking out of the window and I saw Harvey Kimberly walk by and I thought my God how straight like a die he does walk and he's seventy odd. Now if he looks like that so must we and if we look like that then we shouldn't be stuck in this house all the rest of our lives. We've got children we love and who love us and we've got grandchildren we love and who love us and they're all over the place doing all manner of wonderful things and we should go and visit them. I want to know what exactly they're up to. So do you. There's Graeme up in the Orkneys doing research on God knows what. There's Hilda and her husband digging up the past all over the place. I want to see what they're digging up. I've always been interested in digs and old things. Perhaps we can help them. I'd wash clay pots. Lovely. And there's Jake with his business in Hong Kong. I know you were ashamed your only grandson took to business but he is your only grandson and a good boy and it's Hong Kong. Think about it. What's the good of all those savings to us when we're too old to use it that's what I say and you should say it too.

Victor had dozed a little but knew at once when I'd finished. 'She's mad. We've got no savings. A few hundred pounds. Hong Kong! Ha!'

But I joined forces with her: 'She's not simply talking about travel, she's talking about plans to do things and it seems to me that on this hope of a new drug ...'

'What new drug? It's not been tried yet. It might be "that old drug." And *what* plans? I've *got* plans. I want to write this book. What should I want to travel for? Haven't I done enough of that sort of thing? I'm tired now. Stupid woman!'

Outside, the broom, the rhododendrons and the azaleas were on the turn from bud into blossom. It was a bright day but blowy with sunlight switched on and off swiftly by fast blown clouds. 'She hated me being a trade-union leader, you know. Hated it. Man as a political or social animal she could never understand. Men were good or bad, selfish or generous, sensible or idiots, never victims. Discussion, debate, the consideration of political

principles – a foreign language! And it used to make her so angry
that I was tied up in it all. Not that I didn't want to involve her –
I did! And in the beginning it was grand. She was curious about
everything. But later she deliberately crept into the background.
The years from forty to fifty were the worst. Like strangers we
were. Hardly spoke. Terrible time, that. At least for *us*, but not –
funny this – not for her. She seemed to grow. In confidence,
cockiness, independence – some bloody thing or other – grow,
mature, takeover. Aye, that was it, she took over, all but me
General Secretaryship, became another woman, formidable, a
huge presence. I couldn't ever laugh while she was around, even
when there was lots to laugh about. She thought me, well, daft,
when I laughed. I must've been the only man whose laughter
attracted his wife's irritation. Of course I laugh loudly when I
laugh, you know – loud, full-blooded. None of your little giggles.
And she'd sit and fume, as though – well I don't know as though
what – as though she felt laughing was undignified, or it didn't
become me. Big trade union man! Important public figure! Or
maybe she just didn't like laughing any more.

'No, it couldn't be that. She laughed herself. A lot actually,
as I think of it, in the early days. At predicaments! That's it! I'm
just remembering. When an innocent bystander was caught up
in someone else's confusion – that! That amused her. Once, when
she was learning to drive, she came out of a side-turning too
quickly and another car, coming across our path and with the
right of way to pass straight in front of us, was forced to turn
right into the street opposite us, which he did and went straight
on. God knows why he didn't stop and tell her off. And she
laughed! She laughed till she ached. "He didn't want to go down
that street," she kept saying, "poor man! he was on his way to one
place and now he's got to go somewhere else!" That *did* amuse
her that did. Laughed till tears came and she looked beautiful
with it. I remember. Radiant. Maybe she just didn't like *me*

laughing. Unhappy people don't like you laughing do they?'

Victor made one last request before I left him that morning: 'I've been making quite a few notes,' he said, 'for that bloody book. They're no good and it's a waste of everybody's time but could you keep the illusion going for me and have them typed, please?'

I took charge of the sheaf of papers through which I flicked. The name of the Dutch artist, Escher, caught my attention. 'You're poking about in obscure corners of the art world,' I said. 'Escher? Taken a liking to him?'

Victor answered wearily: 'No, I haven't taken a liking to him and he's no longer an obscure artist. In fact there's quite a cult growing up around him. Unhealthy it seems to me. Read, you'll see.' I read a paragraph:

> Escher delights in the cheatability of perspective. His is a playful rather than profound art; it tells us more about the decorative aspect of nature than about its mysterious life-force; he reproduces the patterns of man's architecture rather than reflects the passion and personality that made it; there are few living faces in his prints, or human figures. He seems unmoved by what moves man to contort his body or arrange the bones in his face. There's no face weeping, no eyes laughing, no body leaping, no figure suffering. Only the sterile, geometric shapes of life seem to obsess him, not life itself.

He'd been a good pupil, Ruskin flowed through the observations. But 'cheatability?' I asked him. He grinned. 'And why not, lad, eh?'

'You're a very remarkable man, Victor,' I told him, 'wasted on union matters.'

'Wasted? You think so? You're charitable, Maurice, charitable. But the men had to be protected. You should have seen some of the employers I had to protect them from. Wished they hadn't needed protection, looked after their own bloody selves. But there it is. Done now.'

That day, on leaving him, I went through a strange and rather shaming experience. Driving off in the car I switched on the radio at the moment the Janacek Symphonietta was at its height – a passage full of tall mountains and echoes – and immediately I swung into happy accompaniment, singing with the orchestra. A sense of elation overwhelmed me. I sang loudly, and smiled. It was many minutes before I realized I'd just left the bedside of a dying friend. And then it struck me: I was relieved, deliciously grateful, that someone else was dying and not me, not me!

I was to see Victor alive on only two more occasions, both in the hospital. The first time was three days after he'd been given a bed. Not one adorned with glaring white cushions starched crisp with love and protection against the world, but a metallic thing of cleanliness only.

'It's going to be a long bloody job,' he said, 'longer'n I thought. Longer'n they told me, in fact.'

He was in a ward with one other patient. While I was there the specialist in charge visited him, a brilliant man crippled from polio, with dark eyes, darkened by anxiety for his patients, and a face knotted by constant pain. It was a disturbing, confusing experience to watch him at work. Smiling his pained smile of twin pains, forcing himself to disengage from self-pity to pity for his doomed patients. I hoped, foolishly, that the sight of it would distract Victor from his own distress. But he could be gripped by little of what held the rest of us.

The first thing I did was hand him his notes, typed. He reached for his glasses. But they were of no use. Then his enormous magnifying glass.

'No good,' he said, 'it's no good. I'm going blind. Oh bloody Christ! Maurice.'

I tried, clumsily, to change the subject. 'They're good notes, Victor, fine, fine. Some things I don't agree with, you'd expect that, but it has the makings of a unique little book on art, I promise you.'

It was true, actually. He'd noted down many original observations, though some he'd not been able to substantiate. But I didn't want to over-enthuse for fear of sounding too desperate to be encouraging. Everything must seem patronizing to a dying man.

He was totally indifferent to the book and what I had to say about it.

'Tell me, professor, do you believe in God?'

'I can't,' I replied.

'Right, you can't. Nor can't I. And why? Because we've only got the choice of other men's Gods and if your temperament doesn't fit you can't live with them. Who can live with the God of the Jews, or the Hindus or the Buddhists? So, there you are, facing death, with nowhere to go. And *that's* what I can't accept. I can't believe in an all-powerful God, a one-and-only Creator, but nor can I believe that dying ends it all. Miracles may not make sense but the ceasing forever of all this ... ' Victor knocked angrily on his skull ' ... all this incredible intellect and imagination, that doesn't make sense either.' I wanted to stop and redirect his thoughts but unhappiness gave him momentum; his words bubbled out like hot oil, burning us both, and he spoke to the air not once looking at me or settling his desperate eyes anywhere.

'Of course there are *some* people to whom it makes ecstatic sense, but they're a type, the put-downers I call them. Know who I mean? Any bloody opportunity they get they enjoy putting men down. They have a special tone of voice, the kind of voice that rubs its hands together. "Look at the ocean," they cry, "see what a little thing is man in all that sea!" and when space-rockets came they had a real ball. "Look at all those stars! How insignificant is man now!" Instead of marvelling that man could make it to the bloody moon they found it another opportunity to put him down. And there's those stupid computers. Oh how they do love putting men down because they can't store up facts mechanically. But a computer's a poor thing compared to a brain isn't it? I mean, bloody hell! I'm no scientist but even I know that. Can't store a shred of what the brain can. But on they go. The put-downers! Of which I mercifully have never been one.

'So, there I am – naked. I try to read a book and I can't, because as I'm reading I think: this is going to cease to be able to happen soon. Or I put these earphones on to listen to music and I start crying because I think: soon I'm not going to be here to listen to that. And I look around and I register everything and I think I'm soon never, never, never going to see any of that again. And it doesn't make sense. It just doesn't make sense. I *know* it's going to happen, I *know* it because I've seen death happen and nothing's ever stopped it happening, but it just doesn't make sense. And because it doesn't make sense it seems unjust. The poets were right, *they* knew, unjust! No reason for it! I mean what have I done to have all those bloody marvellous things taken away from me? What? what, what, for Christ's sake?'

The outburst wrung me unbearably. I wanted to talk like a schoolmaster and say stupid things like 'pull yourself together! dignity! self-respect!' And perhaps in such times that's exactly what one *should* say. Righteous or not, perhaps sternness is of great help. But half of me screamed *with* him at the injustice. It *was* unjust, he was right to rage so. In this way empathizing friends are paralysed. It was better to remain silent. He handed me a letter on blue paper.

You took me and you shaped me and you gave me form.
Not a form I couldn't be but the form I was meant to be.
You needed only to be in the house and I felt my life and

the lives of the children I cherished could never go wrong. It was so. They never did go wrong. They have confidence and pity and daring in them. And in me there are flowers. Blossoming all the time. Explosions of colour and energy. You see it, surely? Surely you see it? Or feel it? There's nothing I couldn't do. In me is you. All you've given me. I've been a white sheet, a large white canvas and you've drawn the world upon me, given outline to what was mysterious and frightening in me. Do you know how proud I've been of you? Do you know I've felt myself beautiful only because you chose me? Do you know that I've shuddered with pleasure to think *you* loved *me*? You are my rock my hero my love. I feel such strength. Do you know these things?

'She's going mad, isn't she?' said Victor. His eyes were still unable to settle anywhere. 'They've drugged me you know. Tried to keep me calm. But I'm fighting it. Fighting it hard. I heard what they do in hospitals. Slowly kill the incurables. Pretend it's a nerve-settler. Can't trust them you know.'

I brought him back to his notes and read out passages I thought he'd like to reconsider. For a while he became involved and we talked about art and politics.

Five days later on my next visit he was a changed man. The decline had been rapid and inescapable. A blood drip hung by his side, he was propped up high on his metal bed, a certain stillness was in his eyes. He nodded to the bottle of blood.

'Have to renew it every three hours. Stop the flow and I die. Look at it! A bottle of someone else's blood, just that red stuff in there to keep me able to see you and talk and think and remember and reason. That's it, Maurice, isn't it? The end. Oh, don't protest, lad. I don't think I mind now all that much. In fact, I've got back me curiosity. Who's been right? I may be finding out, you know.

In fact I'm convinced that somehow I'm going to be able to watch it happen and then be around after it's happened. Anyway, around or not, that's it.'

He shifted a little. 'Bloody bed-sores. I've got a rubber ring under my backside but it makes no odds. Lying horizontal still stops the blood circulating.'

He grimaced and a second of rage upped in him, a small blaze of anger. But only a second, then quietly he continued: 'You know what's helped? I woke up the other day and I asked my neighbour over there to read me the newspaper and as he was reading I realized how totally ill-equipped I'd always been to have an authoritative opinion on anything. Facts! Details! Who knows all the facts about anything? And he read and he read until I said to him – no! I can't! And then, out of the blue, no connection at all, I thought: Leonardo Da Vinci is dead. And that seemed re-assuring. So I went on: Mozart is dead, Socrates is dead, Shake-speare, Buddha, Jesus, Gandhi, Marx, Keir Hardie – they're all dead. And one day Sonia will die, and my son, Graeme, he'll be dead, and my daughter, Hilda, and their son Jake, and so will all the grandchildren. And there seemed a great unity to all this. A great simplicity. Comforting.'

He really did seem to have drawn comfort from these thoughts. A lovely beatific calm settled in his eyes. But it ebbed and soon he looked tired, surrendered, a face bleached of all further hope or expectation. The calm eyes turned dull and he slowly wheeled them on me to catch me registering all that was happening, a thing it was impossible not to do and the doing of which was final proof to him that he was right: it was the end. He flicked me a nod of confirmation: yes, you're not imagining things, I'm winding down.

For a moment he forgot I was there and his eyes went out of focus and past me. Then he refocused, smiled, said 'poor Maurice' and handed me a letter from Sonia.

Oh my beloved, my dearest dearest one. I have adored you
how I have adored you. Do you know that? That I am full
of you do you? Know it know it that I feel you there as I've
felt my children in me? Your blood in my blood, rivers of
you, spit and breath and piss and sperm all in me. Do you
know it? The sound of your voice your judgments your
praise your love your pity do you know it? My darling oh
my darling. Nothing has been wrong for me and nothing
will be. I will give you my everything cut from me my
everything lips if you want ears breasts heart. All my body's
everything. To flow in you. What nonsense do I write
instead of just I love you and I always have loved you? But
I must catch up on too much silence. So this nonsense this
silliness this too much writing and talking and shouting is all
for you because I can trust it all and anything to you. Don't
you know now what I feel? Can't you feel what I feel
mad old woman that I am now. Can't you understand I
would rip myself apart for you O my beloved O my sweet
sweet sweetest one. Why am I so clumsy? I've always been
so clumsy never graceful as you deserved. Wretched body
wretched heart dull old mind. Not any part of me good
enough for you I know but O I love you love you love you
O my Victor, Victor, love you, Victor, love you, O my
Victor my heart.

He was asleep when I'd finished reading. He'd wake soon I thought.
But he didn't. I left. On my way out I passed Sonia surrounded
by all the children. She was thinner and looking magnificent with
her black hair swept back in a tight bun, and fierce, as though
defiantly gathering strength to be the bridge between the dying
man she was approaching and the living who, it struck me, she had
brought as evidence that sentence of death could not be passed. I
kissed her, hugged her briefly but said nothing and walked out.

Four days later when I arrived at the hospital they told me Victor had died. Half an hour previously. His family was in there, a nurse whispered. Did I want to go in? I said no, I'd wait till they came out. Was I Professor Maurice Stapleton? Yes, I said. She handed me a package, clumsily wrapped in a white paper bag, bound by two wide, brown elastic bands. Victor had left me the notes for his book and the letters from Sonia. Among them the last one he'd received. Like all of them it was on blue paper and had no date, no beginning, no ending.

There will be, my darling one, I know it, a blinding light a painful light when suddenly the lie will fall away from truth. Everything will make its own and lovely sense, trust me trust me. It won't be logical or happy, this sense, but clear. Everything will become clear. Trust me. Contradictions won't cease to be contradictions, I don't say that, but nor will they any longer confuse. I'm not promising all will seem to have been good but evil won't bewilder you as it once did. Trust me I adore you. And with this blinding light will come an ending to all pain. The body's pain the heart's pain the pain in your soul. All in a second. Less than a second. Less than less than a second. I'm sure of it. That's how it will be for us all. I've always known it. No matter how it happens to us. Accident, torture, suddenly at the top of our energies, quietly in bed. There will come this flash, this light of a colour we've never seen before. It's a glorious moment beloved. Even for the simpleton, even for him, his foolishness falls away just as from the madman his madness falls away. In the instant they know death so they know truth. In the blinding light of truth they know death. One and the same. I promise you trust me love O my love O my Victor O my heart.

1973